BREAKING THE FALL

His head lifted from the pillow.

"Who is it?"

It was a smaller voice than I expected, thin and sleep-strangled. Then, a full-voiced, "Who's there?"

But even then, even with the question reverberating, my heart slamming, I remembered how to be invisible, holding my breath. I shrank to nothing.

I could feel his doubt. He saw, but he didn't see. I was there, crouched on the bedroom floor, and yet I was transparent.

The man sat up, and fought the bedclothes, the blanket and the sheet confining him, weighing him down.

I could not stop my arms, my legs. I leaped, my body springing from all-but-invisible to solid, visible, and trapped.

The nightstand drawer rattled behind me, and the hand fumbled, searched, and then, as I half fell down the dim stairs, the hand found what it was looking for.

It was a small sound. It was a tiny, cold click. I had never heard a sound quite like that before, but I knew exactly what it was.

He had a gun.

BREAKING THE FALL

OTHER PUFFIN BOOKS YOU MAY ENJOY

BREAKING THE FALL

MICHAEL CADNUM

PUFFIN BOOKS

PUFFIN BOOKS
Published by the Penguin Group
Penguin Books USA Inc., 375 Hudson Street, New York, New York 10014, U.S.A.
Penguin Books Ltd, 27 Wrights Lane, London W8 5TZ, England
Penguin Books Australia Ltd, Ringwood, Victoria, Australia
Penguin Books Canada Ltd, 10 Alcorn Avenue, Toronto, Ontario, Canada M4V 3B2
Penguin Books (N.Z.) Ltd, 182-190 Wairau Road, Auckland 10, New Zealand

Penguin Books Ltd, Registered Offices: Harmondsworth, Middlesex, England

First published in the United States of America by Viking,
a division of Penguin Books USA Inc., 1992
Published in Puffin Books, 1994

1 3 5 7 9 10 8 6 4 2

THE LIBRARY OF CONGRESS HAS CATALOGED THE VIKING EDITION AS FOLLOWS:
Cadnum, Michael
Breaking the fall / by Michael Cadnum.   p.   cm.
Summary: Desperately trying to hold together his disintegrating life,
Stanley allows his friend Jared to draw him into a dangerous game of fear.
ISBN 0-670-84687-2
[1. Games—Fiction. 2. Friendship—Fiction.] I. Title.
PZ7.C11724Br   1992   [Fic]—dc20   92-5829   CIP   AC

Puffin Books ISBN 0-14-036004-2

Printed in the United States of America
Set in Electra

FOR SHERINA

———

The bay if we could see

too beautiful to see.

1

YOU HAVE TO HOLD YOUR BREATH.

After a while you have to breathe, but you can breathe so slowly no one, even someone close enough to touch you, can hear that you are there.

But even then, even with every breath measured and slow, something goes wrong. And all you can think is: *I can't do it.*

It wasn't what I had expected at all.

The house around me was huge. The ceiling was a flat, white slab. The furniture hulked, and the carpet hissed under my feet. The house was big, and it was alive, every shadow trembling.

I knew I couldn't do it. Leave now, I told myself. Back out the side window where you came in. Go.

Now.

But I stayed where I was. Some part of me loved this, and I thought: Jared should see me now. He should see how I steal, invisible, all the way across the floor without making a sound.

See, I would tell him, I can do it after all.

It was my first time. Jared had laughed, but I had told him that I could do it, just as he could, and that I would prove it tonight. He was waiting for me even now, and I could imagine him smoking cigarettes and shaking his head to himself, knowing that I wouldn't be able to play his game.

"Go ahead"—he had smiled, shrugging—"see what it's like."

At the bottom of the stairs I pulled myself to my feet.

I had picked out this house carefully, this big white house with green shutters. That would be my house, I had promised myself. That one, with three chimneys—that's the one I'll steal into. It was the biggest house I knew, and had the greenest, most perfect lawn. It was the kind of house I knew I would never live in.

Jared was right: I did feel alive.

The stairs did not merely creak. They moaned, chirped, boomed out low, big-timbred reports.

My mouth was chalk dust. Maybe they aren't home, I told myself. If they aren't here, it doesn't count. When I tell Jared, he'll laugh. It was one of his rules: if no one's home, it doesn't count.

But if they were gone, then I could leave now, and everything would be all right, until another night. Everything was all right, anyway. There was no question about it. The house was empty.

A wave of relief swept over me, but then I gripped the banister so hard my fingers ached. A voice in me said: you are not going to be so lucky.

When a person makes a sound in their sleep, a word or a sigh, it's as though they aren't human beings anymore, not people at all, but something slow and made of wood, some big beast only half turned into something alive, something stunned and lying there nearly gone.

2

There was a grunt, half-gasp, half-word. Nothing more than that. A mutter, then, and someone swimming through sleep, working in the bedclothes to another position.

I was not lucky tonight, not at all. They were in there, in the bedroom, and I leaned against the wall just outside the bedroom door with a slamming heart.

With a terrible voice in me, not my inner voice at all, and not Jared's, either. Some worse, fanged voice saying: Go on, Stanley. Don't just huddle there. If you're so smart, go right ahead.

Jared knew how to be invisible, but I was an imposter, a fake, playing someone else's game. I didn't have the touch, the magic.

Jared's just down the street, waiting for you, and he knows, even though he was so kind, so reassuring. He knows that you can't do it.

Because you're afraid.

2

OUTSIDE THE BEDROOM I decided I would stay where I was, forever. This was supposed to be the good part: the fear. "You'll love the way it makes you feel," Jared had told me.

I could not hear anything but the thud of my heart and

the high, fine shriek of air escaping through my nostrils.

I needed air. I took several shuddering breaths. I inhaled through my nose and exhaled slowly, hiding my breathing like someone in a pile of dead bodies trying to escape the killers, but even so, my panting was far too loud. Anyone could hear it. I might as well jump up and down, shouting.

"How did it go?" Jared would ask. I could invent an adventure and simply lie, but he would see the truth in my eyes. Jared was one of those people who know, without asking.

My body crept on its own, without any will on my part. I could not stop it. I watched myself ease into a room warm with the big, sleeping bodies.

Stop. Go back. This is the worst thing you could do.

But I was inside now. All the way inside the most intimate chamber.

There were two of them, mountains in the bad light. The sounds of sleep, the slow breathing, so low and long it was like they would never wake again.

My palms were wet. My body was cold. I had to breathe again, and yet I knew that if I exhaled now it would hiss out of me. So I crouched as Jared said I should and let my breath out down by the floor, far from where they might hear, and took in another long drag of air down by the crumpled, tossed-off socks and the great black shoes.

I had to take something, but when I straightened just enough to scan the dresser, I couldn't see anything but a white, gently wrinkled cloth, a kind of tablecloth, and a hairbrush. "We aren't thieves," Jared had always said. "We aren't really taking anything important."

4

The man spoke.

The word was unintelligible, a question of some sort. Maybe a name. Maybe his wife's name, because she sighed a question in return, both of them asleep but knowing each other so well they were talking to each other without waking.

Then the man rolled.

His head was an indistinct shape on the pillow, and he was muttering again. His shoulder was a hulk. He rocked on the edge of sleep, about to slip back away, but something stopped him.

His head lifted.

Jared had told me that if I didn't breathe and I didn't move at all I would be invisible. That was the game: being invisible. Invisible like a ghost, and I stayed where I was and thought, you can't see me. You can't. You try, but your eyes can't take me in—because I'm not here.

The head fell back to the pillow. Then—the slightest sound. Not at all a sound, really. But something beyond hearing, something deeper than thought, an awareness of something happening in the bed, something from the bulk of the head on the pillow.

The eyes. It was impossible. It couldn't be true. Surely I couldn't hear them blinking. Surely I couldn't feel the weight of their gaze on me.

I'm invisible. I'm holding my breath, so I'm invisible and you can't see me.

"Who is it?"

It was a smaller voice than I expected, thin and sleep-strangled. Then, a full-voiced, "Who's there?"

But even then, even with the question reverberating, stirring his bedmate into life, my heart slamming, I remembered how to be invisible, holding my breath. I shrank to nothing.

I could feel his doubt. He saw, but he didn't see. I was there, crouched on the bedroom floor, and yet I was transparent, an illusion.

A woman's voice, sleep-clouded, asked, "What is it?"

The man sat up, and fought the bedclothes, the blanket and the sheet confining him, weighing him down.

I could not stop my arms, my legs. I leaped, my body springing from all-but-invisible to solid, visible, and trapped. But I was too slow. The air was water, and my bones were made of heavy, dark stone, each foot dragging.

It was not even fear that froze the man and woman exactly as they were, tangled in the sheets. It was pure incomprehension. They could not believe what they saw.

I swam, clumsier with each heartbeat, along the wall to the black cave of the bedroom door. That was enough: they believed in me now. I knew he was coming after me. I heard the rip of bedding.

The nightstand drawer rattled behind me, and the hand fumbled, searched, and then, as I half fell down the dim stairs, the hand found what it was looking for.

It was a small sound. It was a tiny, cold click. I had never heard a sound quite like that before, but I knew exactly what it was.

He had a gun.

———

3

LOOSE AND FLESHY, the living room carpet held my feet, and the black electrical cords seemed to writhe, tripping me. The window, the open sash, and the parted curtain far across the room shrank as I stumbled, lunged, gasped my way to the sill.

His steps thundered on the stairs.

My shoulders, my butt, the backs of my thighs had high, keen, tickling wounds where I imagined, and nearly felt, the bullets rip me.

And yet there were no shots, not even when I wormed and hung from the window, the night air on my face. I blinked at the surprising breeze that had risen, shaking the great column of a juniper beside one of the chimneys.

Jared had always said that there was a way to fall so it wouldn't hurt, a way to break the fall and roll away, uninjured. There is never any reason, Jared said, for a person to be hurt.

I fell.

I sprang to my feet, the lawn squeaking under my soles. I knew that I was free even as I knew that this was all too late, all too clumsy, and way too slow. The man had seen me, and even now he would be on the phone. Even now a black-and-white would squeal around the corner, siren off but lights twirling.

There I would be, bounding, panting across the front lawns, splashing in the gutter, careening into a streetlight, dancing down one alley and up another, taking the long way, because I did not want to lead the cops to Jared.

My body sang inside with the hope that I might make it after all. My bowels were steady now, and I had so much energy, power, pure light in my legs that I knew that if I really wanted to, I could bound over one of these houses.

But that would be a stupid thing to even try. Anyone who saw me would know that I had been up to something very strange. I could imagine the cop voice. "Officer needs assistance. Kid jumping houses on Manzanita Street."

Then I could barely run at all, knowing even as a stitch bit into my side and my lungs burned that to run now was the worst thing I could do. Anyone could tell at a glance.

Slow down. Walk. Catch your breath.

Then you can circle back to Jared. What was I going to say to him? I didn't have to tell him anything. I could keep this to myself. "Hey, Jared, I decided against trying it tonight. It was windy all of a sudden and I figured people would be awake because of the wind. . . ."

As though I could lie. As though I could stare Jared in the face and say something as untrue as that.

The wind tossed a hamburger wrapper across MacArthur. The wind coursed through my hair and fluttered my clothes. The street was composed of islands of light from the streetlights, sodden dark in between. I skirted the patches of light,

8

but when I found myself outside Sky's house, I saw how I had tricked myself.

There was a crack of light under the garage door, but the house was dark, slumbering. It was, after all, well past midnight.

Someone was working in the garage, her dad or her brother. I could hear a radio, music I could not make out, and I could not guess why I stepped to the front porch and put my hand to the rail.

The rail might have been cold, as everything else was cold that night, but to me it felt warm. Sky's house. My lips actually shaped the words.

She was in there. Right in there.

The date palm in the front yard made a long, ragged whisper in the wind, and a palm frond rattled, dropping nearby, a gray, ghostly shape, a giant feather. The lawn was pebbled with old date pits from the tree, and I found myself unable to leave.

Stay here. Stay here where the living people are, sleeping or studying or working on their cars, wrapped in their lives.

Here where people are happy.

But Jared was waiting, and when I trotted up the street where I had left him, I paused by the green NOT FOR DEPOSIT OF MAIL postal box and made a short whistle. It was a terrible little whistle, like the cheep of a sick finch.

The bottle brush plant made the slightest shift to one side, and his cigarette was a chip of fire. He laughed. He was actually laughing in his silent way.

He didn't even have to ask.

4

"IT'S ALL RIGHT. You did very well. For a beginner."

We were back in Jared's house, in Jared's room, and the wonderful power in my legs was gone. There was a taste in my mouth like ash.

I thought: there'll be a knock at the door downstairs, interrupting the party of sophisticated people, some of them speaking French and Russian.

The faraway laughter was a little too loud. It was very late and the party was getting a little drunk and shabby.

"No, really," Jared consoled me, even though he laughed as he said it. "It wasn't your game, after all. It's mine. You shouldn't have tried to do it all by yourself. I was wrong to encourage you." He gestured at me like a magician: presto, now you're happy. He was thin and dark-haired, and knew how to speak with his eyes, and with his hands.

He laughed silently and shook his head. "I was nervous the first time, too," he said. He smiled at me through the smoke. He waved a hand, in his grand way. "They won't hurt you," said Jared.

"I know it," I said, but I knew that what I meant was: they won't hurt *you*, but they'll hurt *me*. And I hated the little rasp in my voice, the dry croak I made.

I was so ashamed—and so shaken—that my lower lip was

trembling. I have my moments of minor courage. I played shortstop, and if I couldn't get the ball in my glove, I stopped it with my face. I heard things like, "Way to go with the face, Stan." "Great face, Stanley."

There was a flare of adult laughter downstairs. Jared's parents were sitting around sucking drinks with other smart people, people in tweed and cufflinks, gin drinkers.

I glanced around his bedroom. A carton of Marlboros was open on the dresser, and the room was a tumble of books and clothes, some of them shirts still wrapped in plastic from the department store. On the wall Jared had a map of the night sky at midwinter, a delicate tracing of Orion and Taurus, and several pinups of the sort my parents would never have allowed, tousled women with blossoming labia and hard gazes. There was a dark spill of marijuana on the nightstand. "Nobody cares," Jared had told me once, "what I do."

And he had his trophies, a tangle of them there in his bedroom, on the dresser: a lighter, a gold pen, a box of oversized plastic paper clips—all of the curios, knickknacks he had stolen not for their value, although some of the objects did look expensive. They were proof that he had crept into the innermost room of a house, and snatched a token, any random object, as proof.

It was a secret game Jared had played all by himself, until at last he had begun to hint around about it, saying, "I know a game that most people would be too scared to even contemplate."

Jared used words like *contemplate* easily. His father was the author of books about astronomy, and was always flying

11

off to Arizona or Hawaii to visit observatories where men and women like him studied the stars. His mother did technical drawings at the university, precise representations of the jaws of extinct rodents and the fangs of long-lost birds, and she, too, was always flying off to conferences in far-off cities.

Jared knew things. He didn't just have facts straight, numbers ready, dates and famous writers. He knew things like that. But what was remarkable was that he made no mistakes. None. If Jared decided to walk along the top of the chain-link fence beside the DANGER HIGH VOLTAGE signs—and he did this often—he would never slip. Never falter. Never hesitate for an instant, unless he wanted to pretend to be about to fall in the way that made me scream inside myself and put my hand out to the fence and draw myself into one tight thought: don't die, Jared.

Don't die.

Once he walked across the 580 Freeway, on the pedestrian walkway over eight lanes of traffic. He goat-footed his way along the top of the suicide cage, the fence that arches over the walkway to keep people from doing just what Jared had decided he would do. It was exactly his style: watch what I can do.

But gradually, very slowly, our new friendship became more than a shared midnight laugh, more than me watching Jared teeter along one fence, more than a matter of watching Jared bound across traffic while cars squealed.

"It's better than any drug," he would say with a smile, and he had tried them all. "It's better than sex," he would say, and he knew all about that, being muscular and bored-looking

12

enough to have a girl on each arm sometimes after school.

At first I didn't believe him. "You don't really," I said. "Not really."

He made one of his gestures. Jared could say as much with a shrug, a wave, as most people could with whole conversations, complete with charts and pointers. So don't believe me, his shrug said. I care nothing what you believe or don't believe. Be a little, dull person. What do I care?

Of course, that was only a joke. Jared wouldn't really hurt anyone, or even take anything especially important. His game was, in a way, an act of mercy. He would slip into a house, hold the lives within his power—and spare them.

I sat in his bedroom, a friend who had failed, and Jared was kind, tossing me the pack of cigarettes and the gold-plated—stolen—Zippo. It was an old-fashioned kind of lighter, and I tossed it in my hand for a moment, thinking: the person who lost this misses it.

"Maybe next time I'll go with you, back to the same house. It sounds like an interesting challenge. A creaking staircase." He widened his eyes, as though to mock me. "A gun in the nightstand."

"They'll be ready for you," I said.

"For us," he said.

I'm never going back there, I told myself. Never.

"All it takes is the right touch." Jared leaned back in his chair, watching the smoke from his cigarette drift toward the ceiling. "It'll be all the more fun. Burglar alarms, brand-new rented guard dogs."

Never, I wanted to say. Not as long as I live. It would be

a disaster. I would slow him down, and my doubt, my clumsy lack of faith, would ruin everything.

But Jared read my thoughts.

He wasn't smiling. "I've decided. Next time," he said. "We'll do it together."

5

THE FRONT DOOR was not locked when I reached my own house off Park Boulevard. I froze for a second, thinking: a break-in.

Someone's in there, a burglar.

I did not move, listening, even sniffing the air, trying to see through the walls of my house. Oakland is beside San Francisco Bay, and often smells of smog mixed with a kind of fog no one can see, a wet breath that chills everything. The background noise is always a grumble of traffic, a steady freeway rumble in the distance.

My own house was so still after the chatter and chiming ice cubes of Jared's house that the fear flashed back, all over my body. I leaned against the jamb for a moment.

Surely, I told myself, it was impossible. Had I really entered someone's house?

It was leftover fear, excess adrenaline. There was no one

here, hiding in my house. I was being silly. I pushed the door, and it swung almost silently, with only the barest, breathy whine of its hinges.

My breath caught.

My dad was sitting in the living room, gazing at the television, which was not on. He held a beer in his hands, but the beer was not open. The light at his elbow was the only light on in the house, illuminating an unopened *Wall Street Journal* on the table at his elbow.

But it was only my father. His arrival was always hard to predict, but there was no reason why the sight of his profile should startle me.

He spoke to me after I had passed. "What's up, Stanley?" he said.

I came back into his presence, and he found me with his eyes. His gray suit was rumpled, his new red tie unknotted, the thin half flung up across his shoulder. His briefcase was on his lap, unopened.

"Out late," he said. It was his usual way of asking a question, even making an accusation.

"The Trents had a party."

"A party," said my father, not a question—an acknowledgment. "That's good," he said, reflecting on what I had said. "Did you talk to anyone interesting?"

"There were Russians."

He stirred, blinking. He had kept awake only as long as he had because worry had pricked him and kept him there.

"Astronomers from Russia?"

"I guess so."

"Figuring out the universe." He said this without sarcasm or cynicism. My father works at a foundry, but instead of making manholes or drop-forged can openers, he balances the books and runs the computer that cranks out the paychecks. The foundry is just about broke. My father keeps the factory in business by sitting at his desk in the factory office with a calculator. He lives on aspirin.

My mother has a similar job, doing, as she puts it, "everything," but her calendar takes her to Chicago and Boca Raton to drink coffee with people who design computers. My mother knows how to help software companies save costs. She had just bought a twelve-hundred-dollar briefcase, and was spending the night in Seattle.

Her absence stepped into the room like a spirit, a new, worse kind of silence for a moment. "Homework," said my father.

"I'm caught up." I added what was not a lie. "Jared helps me with the math."

"That's good." Again, no irony, nothing arch or insincere. My father wanted me to go to college, and he had always encouraged me to spend time with Jared and his parents. "Don't live the way I do," he had told me once, drunk with paperwork, closing his eyes so he wouldn't have to see his laptop with its deep blue screen and rows of silver numbers. "Do something wonderful with your life."

He broke the silence as I was about to leave. "She left a message on the machine."

"Is she having a good time?"

An idle question, an exit line, but it was the wrong thing to say.

Lately I had begun to wonder. I was wondering right then, and my father didn't like me thinking about her. We probably shared the same thoughts.

He cleared his throat. "You ate?" he asked.

"A burrito with Jared."

"I couldn't find the Weenie." He meant the gizmo that turned on the television, which he called the Magic Weenie. And his words were a kind of shorthand. He meant: I couldn't get Ruth on the phone. He also meant: I'm worried about you.

For some reason I asked him a question I had never asked him before in my life. "Did you have supper?"

He stirred, perhaps surprised at my question. "I more or less forgot."

"You can't forget something like that. You'll get an ulcer."

I was about to add, "I'll make you something," envisioning a can of chili, or a microwave Salisbury steak, when he said, "There was a lot of unusual paperwork."

His tone told me more than his words.

"A bad day," I suggested.

"Oh," he sighed, a long vowel that told me he could not talk about his work, its labors, its boredom. But he surprised me. "There was an accident. A guy died."

"Died?" My father never talked about the factory.

"A guy I knew to say hi to. A nice guy. A bunch of pipe rolled on him."

17

Words vanished. I must have said something like, "That's awful."

"Yes," he said slowly, gazing at the empty screen. He didn't talk for a long time. "Stanley," he said, as though my name were the answer in a guessing game he was desperate to win.

I meant to say something to cheer him, to reassure him.

Before I could speak, he said, "I want you to take care of yourself."

WHEN I WAS IN BED, after I had fixed us some Weight Watchers lasagna, and after my father's shower, I lay awake in what was left of the night. My father's words kept plodding back into my mind.

Not "a mountain of pipe collapsed." Not "an avalanche of iron." My father never dressed up the truth. Some pipe had rolled; a man was gone.

I lay, staring at the blank ceiling, praying that everyone I knew would be safe, knowing how selfish this was. My parents were merely two humans in a world crowded with people.

May my mother come home safely on the plane, and may my father be safe.

And then I prayed that Jared would think of another game to play.

———

18

6

MY MOTHER NEVER LOOKS AT YOU when she talks to you. It's as though we're always on an assembly line putting together telephones or video machines and have to keep concentrating on our work.

It was Monday morning, two days after my failure. Seattle had been a bitch, my mother said, which meant either that she had been very successful after a lot of trouble, and wanted a round of applause from me, or that Seattle had been a disaster and was beneath the level of civilized conversation.

My first impression was that my father had left before either of us had crawled downstairs, but I tucked in my shirt and realized that things were not that simple. My mother looked fresh, and she had plainly been up for a long time. I was used to quiet, and quiet people. It made me aware of the different kinds of silence.

Sometimes I thought I heard them having sex. I wasn't sure. But a couple of times in my life I had awakened suddenly, certain that a voice had called out a name. Or not even a name—just a cry, like someone awakened with a syllable on her lips. This night had been dreamless, and I had almost overslept. But something had happened. The house looked smaller, and a sweater I had never seen before

19

hung on the back of a chair. It was a black sweater, a woman's cashmere. And my father's toast crust was at my elbow.

"Eat more than a banana," she said, adjusting her pantyhose through her skirt, a motion a little like a hula.

"Bananas have potassium. Bananas are the perfect food. You can't eat anything better than a banana," I said, and then I shut up for a moment.

"So Seattle was horrible," I added after a while, in my father's half-statement, half-question tone.

I knew it bothered her when I began a question with *so*. It's a way of dismissing everything that has been said and done, as though the following words are the point of the entire conversation.

"I killed them," she said. She messed up the line with her overprecise enunciation. Not "I killed 'em."

"Figuratively," I responded, hating to sound so much like my father.

A little nonlaugh as she stirred her coffee.

I hunched against the kitchen door, gazing back at her. I didn't have to ask. Perhaps it was the way she acted: when she was here she was always just recovering from one of their talks, or getting ready for another one. She and my father had spoken the night before, or even early that morning. It had been a hard conversation, one easy to imagine. Short sentences and long silences. Now she was off-duty, stuffing toast into the slots. The television news was on. That meant you never had to talk in the mornings. You could always become absorbed in the national weather.

20

I was wondering, though, how my mother might look to a man her own age. Whether she was pretty. She had dark, very curly hair, almost nappy hair, and long, thin arms. At a Christmas party once, champagne-bright, she had said she was part everything: Cherokee, Irish, Armenian, Spanish.

She watched the toaster, and the toaster made a click, and then a wrinkle of heat danced above it, as always when the toast was about to pop.

My mother played a lot of tennis, and watched videos of tennis stars talking about how to serve. She would practice in front of the television, serving with an imaginary racket. She was always happy when she came back after playing at Strawberry Canyon. Before I hurt my leg, she and I would go to the courts and hit the ball back and forth, informally. I think we were both sure the other would win if we kept score. She played a lot better than I did, although I wasn't bad. Sometimes I would win a compliment from her on my backspin.

"New dress," I said.

"Skirt," she answered.

I held the swinging door open with my weight and, after a while, it seemed to want to shut. It continued to grow heavier as I stood there. "It looks nice," I said.

She looked at me for the first time, with the slightest of smiles, and I saw that she was, really, pretty. "Silk/wool," she said. A little laugh again, remembering, perhaps, the store, or the price. "Sinful."

You didn't have to see it on the five minutes of local news

beside the toaster. She was on her way. Seattle had been wonderful for her. She didn't even look tired. She was going places.

MY GOAL FOR TODAY was to avoid Jared, and my second goal was to talk to Sky again, because for all my faith in her—and that's what it was, faith—I had spoken to her only from time to time, just to say hello. She had watched me play baseball, when I was still playing, including one or two real terrible plays, one of my Face Specials, my eye socket as a sort of secondary fielder's glove.

Today would be an important day. That was what I promised myself. All I had to do was talk to Sky, and Jared—surely I could avoid him.

He was waiting for me somewhere. I would see him soon, leaning against a telephone pole or slouching out of a 7-Eleven. He wouldn't call out. He would smile, and he would shake out a cigarette for me, and I would take it.

I couldn't help it. I wanted to impress Jared. I wanted that more than anything. But I wanted something else.

I wanted that fear again, that fear that finally turned to light.

I wanted to feel alive.

———

7

THE NEW SCHOOL was right across the football field from where the old one had blown up. The old school had been a craggy, castlelike building, ugly but impressive, as though a high school might be attacked by something supernatural, a dragon or a giant.

The new Wilson School was a series of low buildings with flat roofs, gray and off-gray. You saw the backboards of the basketball court and the big yellow loop of the track around the football field before you saw the buildings. If these walls collapsed they wouldn't hurt anyone. You'd shake them off like so much bulletin board material that had just happened to fall down.

Some people liked sitting in the buildings, but everyone with lungs and blood in their bodies stayed out on the football stands. There was always something to watch. There were fights, and you could watch the drug corner across the street—even on the days when the cops staked it out, expensive cars cruised by.

Before school I sat exactly as I always did, smoking with Jared. Jared stubbed his cigarettes out on the heads of the bolts that held the bleachers together. That way the yellow paint didn't get charred.

"The same house," he said, standing up.

"With the green shutters," I said, as though in agreement.

"Tonight." He smiled.

"Not tonight," I began. A half-dozen excuses crowded me. "Maybe this weekend," I offered feebly.

"You'll just get more and more nervous. It's best to get it over with."

He put a forefinger on the knuckle of my hand, just a touch, as though to push a switch to activate my brain. I shrugged, the way he often did, as though it made no difference to me at all. This was what I wanted, I told myself. The game was life. And this—this was hardly life to me, the sound of the bell barely leaking all the way to the muddy football field, the scraps of old daily bulletins plastered against the chain-link fence.

But the thought had given my mouth a sour taste.

Not tonight. Not the same house. It was crazy.

MR. MILLIKEN DECIDED to spend the entire period lecturing on the steam engine. He was a round, red-haired man, with white curls of hair on his freckled arms. "They would blow up," he exclaimed, "scalding hundreds!"

He stalked the room like a giant zombie. "Painful, howling deaths! Steamboats blowing up on the Mississippi! Locomotives blowing up in the station! These were dangerous machines. Even when they didn't explode, they rained hot cinders. Blinding ashes! Stanley!" he exclaimed.

He did this to make sure we were listening. "We the People, in order to Stanley," he might say, just to make sure I was listening, and I always was, but years of living with my mother have accustomed me to listen without looking.

I looked at him and waved, a little sarcastically. He gave a frowning smile in return. He taught history as a series of lurid headlines. As a result, we were way behind schedule. I could hardly wait for the Civil War.

Sky Tagaloa was in this class. Her long dark hair was held together with a little blue elastic like a miniature bungee cord.

As we were tumbling out of class Mr. Milliken put a big freckled hand on my shoulder. "You look a little sleepy there, North."

I didn't respond, so he said, "Wake up or stay home."

I shrugged, and did my gimme-a-break smirk. I was happy to slip away from him, and trudge just behind Sky past the slamming lockers.

I said hello to her as she found her locker and spun the dial. "Hello, Stanley," she said. She had a deep voice, and always spoke slowly.

Hello, Stanley. She had said as much before. She had been friendly enough. *Hello.* She had repeated my greeting back to me. And she hadn't said "Stan." She had used my whole name, both syllables. I liked that—I hated to be called Stan.

But my plan was not going well. We had always been on speaking terms. This was not an improvement. This morning was turning out to be just another dead day. A dead day in a school with air conditioning that sucked the oxygen out of the rooms.

25

And the day chugged forward, dead, flat, dull.
Until lunch. Then everything changed.

8

IT WAS NOON, and the sun was that same rotten smear in the sky.

I was sitting off to the side, as usual, waiting for Jared to get done talking to the dean or the counselor or whomever else he had gotten himself tangled with this time. A big, broad guy sauntered across the field to get from MacArthur to Blake Avenue, rolling a little, like he was feeling his liquid brunch just about then.

He hooked Sky's backpack with one hand, as an afterthought, maybe, or maybe an old habit that was hard to break. She had turned to look back at the building, and the man's easy snatch of the pack looked like something done as a joke.

She turned and felt her shoulder, felt her arm, even as she watched the guy take her pack, watched the strap glide off her arm and wrist. Her lips parted, about to smile or begin some kind of rejoinder, and she actually said, with some humor, "Hey, wait a minute—"

And then she saw it wasn't a joke. This guy was a stranger,

and he was big, and starting a slow lope, good-humored and loose, like he thought it was a joke, too.

Sky had some trouble finding a place on the forty-yard line to drop her French book. Everything was wet. Then she slipped a little, and when she finally got her footing I was standing up in the bleachers and thinking, no, Sky, don't go after him. Let it go.

It was a short sprint, and when she caught up with him, he hit her. Casually, glancing back with a wave, like someone gesturing away a gnat. Not hard, sort of a backhand slap, nearly a joke in itself, but you could hear the smack of it all the way over where I was, and I shrank inside at the sound.

Sky had him. She got ahold of his jacket, a gray, zippered windbreaker that was open in front, and swung him around. The guy tried to laugh. He tossed the backpack, and it splashed into a puddle. Look, he said with a gesture, I don't have it anymore. If I don't have it, his expression tried to say, everything's okay, right?

Besides, Sky was having trouble spinning him to the ground. The jacket stretched out, half-pulled off the guy, and the guy was rotating on one foot, but Sky wasn't exactly making a clean tackle. The day had stopped, and no one could move or even make a sound, except the two who seemed joined together.

The light changed. The bleary sunlight was even more glaring, half fog, half mist, and my own feet splashed in the wet mud. The stranger was almost entirely out of his jacket, an escape artist, when he seemed to grow bigger. His shoulders swelled, and his neck muscles bunched and he knotted his hands into fists.

His fist made a bone-on-bone *thwack* against her head, and then another, with a motion like someone wielding a hammer. He spread his feet to plant them well, those invisible nails, but Sky was not letting go, not crying out at all.

She was moving in on the guy, her face crumpled with shock. She grappled with him, and it was this embrace that slowed down the stranger, and pinned his arms, until I found myself with my own arms around one of his legs.

Something out of television football, years of instant re-plays, must have been encoded in what I was doing. My feet tore the grass, driving forward, and the man actually left the ground, his weight on my back, heavier and harder than I had dreamed it would be.

They both fell, and the force of the fall separated them. The stranger smiled, a smart I'm-okay twist to his face. He stood up in stages, planting a foot, pulling himself up, flicking grass off his knees. He glanced at Sky, and then he smiled at me, and I thought—it's okay. It's really okay. He's taking it as a joke.

He kicked me. I saw the foot retreat, and I saw it loom in my eyes, and the world contracted to a little circle of blue and green. The dark, muddy shoe burst into my skull, and a single blue star flashed for an instant in my vision.

He kicked me again, a noise like two boulders clunking together.

I saw what happened next as though I existed on another planet. Trying to climb out of the muck and grass clippings,

I watched on my own little television, the little screen that perched right before my eyes, all I could make out of the world.

A new figure joined us. A new, big shape fell from the sky. He was there, suddenly, and he dropped on the guy, actually leaped, flew through the air and flattened the stranger with a whoosh of air and a gristly, butcher-shop snap.

It was all quiet.

Then the rescuing figure ascended to his feet, and I recognized Tu, Sky's brother. He marched upon me, all bulk and white teeth.

I flinched.

He put his arm all the way around me. "Hey! Get this guy some water!" he called, illogically, perhaps remembering the line from a movie. "Fuck!" called Tu, who always swore awkwardly. "Some water for this guy!" he called, and I was certain he was about to lift me like a trophy.

Behind us, off to one side, the stranger dragged himself together and began his fade from the field.

Sky looked me in the eyes. Looked right into my eyes, with her face close to mine.

"Stanley," she said, in her slow, gentle voice, not even breathing hard. "Are you all right?"

"This guy!" cried Tu, and his words were like the cry of a man who has made a wonderful discovery. "Let us through with this guy," said Tu as we shouldered our way to the nurse's office, where I sat with Tu pounding my back and Sky watching me from the doorway as though she had never really seen me before, as though she realized after all this

29

time that I was someone she used to know, in another world, in another life, and that she had been a fool not to recognize me before now.

9

AFTERNOON IS MY FAVORITE PART of the day. In the afternoon there is an island of an hour or two, an extra day in the day.

In the afternoon streets look like friendly places, ways to go from one place to another. A city has houses, fences, bushes, and the trees that expand into the sky and give a feeling that the world is a refuge. By day this is all our home, every grocery store, every parking lot, a way for people to live and find their lives.

But at night, outside, when the streetlights are not strong enough to dilute the dark, the streets are another, foreign place. The world is not our home after all.

My father was not home for supper, as usual, and my mother came home as I was making a show of going to bed. She unpacked her briefcase and scattered papers all over the desk in the crowded sewing room she used as an office. When I stepped into the room to say good night, she was eating a Burger King cheeseburger, a ragged tendril of lettuce hanging onto her spreadsheet.

She did not look up as she said, "Are you okay?"

"Sure."

"You're so . . ." She hunted for a word while stapling two pages together. "Thin."

I wasn't really thin, no more than usual. But it was typical of my parents. They were buried by their work, but from deep within the heap of paperwork, I always heard the injunction to take vitamin C, or not to take out the trash in my bare feet.

Besides, there was something changed about me. I could tell, and anyone who saw me could tell. Maybe that beast in me, that hunting creature, was gradually taking over my body.

"Did you eat the beef burgundy?" she was asking.

"I had some eggs."

"Look in the freezer, Stan. I always leave you something." She looked at me then, peering hard before she glanced away. She did not look as pretty as she had. She had lost weight herself, it seemed, and there was a little wrinkle on each side of her mouth. "Homework?"

"Sure."

"What was it?" she asked.

"French. A quiz tomorrow. U.S. History. Read a chapter." I shrugged, to say: just standard homework.

"If you're smart," she said cryptically, "people just expect you to do more work."

I turned to leave, but her voice stopped me, chilling me.

"I know what you've been doing."

I could not make a sound.

"You know how I feel about it."

31

I could not even clear my throat.

"Cancer," she said. "Of the lung."

I was frail with relief. "I don't," I managed to say, "inhale that much."

She let that pass without comment, no doubt recognizing a lame remark. "Don't stay awake all night listening to music."

For a while I lay on the bed in my clothes. Then I did something I had never done before. I escaped my house, like a convict, hanging from my window, landing easily on the laundry room roof, and springing to the back lawn. The easiness of it made me feel all the more guilty. I could not shake it: this was wrong.

There was a fluttering in my belly. All of this was wrong. An appetite had been awakened, though, that only one thing could satisfy.

I met Jared at the bottle brush plant. We crouched in the chilly dark, out of the wind, and smoked. We didn't say much at first. Jared squatted, peering at the street, and while I could not see his face clearly in the bad light, I did not have to.

"I heard you were hurt," he said, standing up.

It was hard to think of the best way to put it. "Kicked in the head."

"In the head?" He sounded amused, and something in me stiffened. "But you are all right," he added more kindly, "obviously."

I did have a lump just above my hairline, and if I shook my head very hard, like someone making a milkshake by

32

hand, it would give me a headache. The nurse had suggested aspirin after I said that she had five fingers and that I did not feel like throwing up.

"I hear," he said without looking back, "that you're a big hit with the Samoans."

For some reason I did not want to say any more about it, so I kept my silence. I followed him down the slope, and we both hurried along the sidewalk. I did not want to describe to Jared what had happened, and I did not want to mention Sky.

I was almost hoping that Jared would suggest some other house, or another plan altogether. We were going down an alley, not a trashy, puddle-strewn alley, but a well-ordered back passage with white paint on the telephone poles up to head height, and red reflectors on the gate posts.

The house loomed over the fence. The hulk of its roof was dark. The three chimneys were sharp black shapes.

That voice was back, the dry, fanged voice in me: you remember this place, said the voice with a kind of glee.

This was the house. This was the place I had promised myself I would never visit again.

"It's too early," I whispered.

"It's an appropriate hour. Past midnight."

But there was a light on upstairs, a dull copper glow. I pressed my eye to a crack in the fence. The wood was new, and a bead of sap kissed my cheek. There was another, brighter light downstairs.

"They expect us," Jared breathed.

My stomach was a knot.

33

"They've gone to bed," he said, with something like sat-isfaction, "but they're nervous."

I don't blame them, I thought, my spit drying to nothing.

"A challenge," he said, and his smile flashed in the dark-ness. He put both hands on the top of the fence and was over it in an instant. He hissed at me through the fence, "Come on."

Stay where you are, I told myself. Stay right here. Let Jared do whatever he wants to do. It has nothing to do with you.

But the fear was already working in me, like the yellow pills Jared and I had taken one Saturday, giving me a feeling of power that made my heart hammer. This fear was what I hated, and what I craved.

The fear itself pulled me over the fence, where I followed Jared toward the great, unsleeping citadel of the house.

10

FROM THE START there was something wrong.

There was danger here, greater than before.

And yet from the beginning the danger only made the darkness sweeter.

The back door was not locked, but a chain kept it from opening more than a few fingers wide. A kitchen window eased upward for a few heartbeats and then stopped. Another window pushed upward, too, but when I shouldered Jared up to it, I could feel him shake his head, the movement communicated throughout his body, a tremor: *no*.

I was sick deep inside, in my stomach, where there was something cold and dead. Cold and dead, but stirring, aroused to life. The windows opened easily. They weren't locked. They weren't locked at all.

And they should have been.

I was alive again. Those gray, fuzzy hours in the classroom, those nights lying drowsy in my bed, those endless conversations, the books, the television—it was all nothing. There was nothing else that made me feel so close to my own heartbeat.

Nothing else lifted me like this. This, I saw, was what I really wanted. Smells were fresh, sounds were vibrant. This was what it was to be alive—alive as cats were, and hunting hawks, alive like the owl, gliding, seeing everything.

It was easy. Jared stood on the gas meter and worked at the window with a long, thin shaft I recognized only after a moment as a screwdriver. He didn't need to break anything— the metal blade was only a lever. The window sighed upward, and then it froze in place.

Jared jumped down and said, "Worm in, Stanley."

Too easy, I wanted to say. I even took in a breath to say the words, "It's a trap."

His voice was a slap: "Be quick."

And I agreed. The danger didn't matter—if anything, it made me more keen. The window sill had been recently painted with a glossy, slick white that let me slide easily. I snaked, worked my arm and shoulder, and then my entire upper body into a room that smelled of laundry detergent.

The floor creaked under me. I caught my breath and listened.

There is no feeling like it; I was where I did not belong. The thought was like a second heartbeat: *Wrong. This is wrong.*

The washing machine reflected the bad light, and seemed to glow. A laundry basket, a skeletal tub made of woven plastic, rested beside me on the floor. There was a breathy presence somewhere off to my left—a water heater.

I opened the window even wider. It shimmied upward, chattering in its wooden runners. Chill air seeped into the warm room. Jared climbed up and in, and his hand sought mine in the half-dark. I gripped it, and steadied him as he sprang to the floor.

The floor did not creak. It made no sound at all.

The linoleum floor had been waxed, and it glistened with a light from somewhere off in the house, a light so bright it leaked all the way to the washer and the dryer, making it easy to see.

He melted to the doorway without a sound. He turned to find me with his eyes. "In a situation like this," Jared said, panting just a little, so that his words were breathy. He was not whispering, daring the house to overhear him. "In a situation like this, we have to be very quick."

He stooped, tucking in his head. He heard something.

We both listened to the purr and sudden silence of a refrigerator. The unseen appliance, far off in the kitchen, gurgled.

He put his hand on my arm, lightly, the kind of touch he might use to soothe a nervous animal. "You stay here."

Prove yourself to Jared, my mind said. He thinks that you are not equal to this.

My voice was still, but he knew my thoughts. His eyes glittered in the bad light. When he spoke next it was a command, devoid of any humor or kindness, but supported by what both of us knew was the truth: "Don't even try, Stanley."

Arguments flowered in me. I could do it. I knew it. He was being unfair. On the other hand, there were hundreds of other houses. There were other nights.

He twitched around the corner and was gone. My body followed him into the kitchen. He did not seem to hear me. When he turned to see me, there was a new look in his eyes, nothing I had seen before.

He was intense, awake. His eyes looked at me not as a friend, not as someone he knew, but as a potential problem, a threat.

I did not read fear in his eyes. It was something cold and even unkind. He didn't want me there. He knew I would slow him down, entangle him in my own inexperience. This look alone was enough to make me shrink to the cold hulk of the refrigerator.

Then Jared's attitude shifted, his wariness melting for a moment. There was the glint of a tooth. He was smiling. He lifted a finger to his lips, and crouched in the doorway. He motioned me forward, and indicated a place in the corridor ahead of us.

A house has a smell, a distinctive atmosphere, and a sound, the nature of the hush the walls throw up against the undercurrent of traffic. I saw nothing. Carpet. A distant doorway, and the feel as well as the sight of the living room that had nearly trapped me as I fled the thudding footsteps.

I felt blank and heavy with stupidity, beastly dumbness, and could not imagine what Jared was trying to tell me.

Then I saw it.

There on the wall was a single, hard red point of light. A bright tiny red star, more scarlet, more fake-gem bright than anything natural. The star glittered alone on a square plate of stainless steel. A key was thrust into the steel plate. A ripple of sensation swept my skin, a feeling nearly like pleasure. I could not name what I saw, but I understood what it was.

Something knew we were there.

11

JARED PUT HIS HAND over my mouth, stifling what I was about to say.

His lips met my ear. "They are already on their way."

I shivered, all the way through my body.

He whisper-answered a question I had not asked: "Silent alarm."

I had guessed that it was a silent alarm, of course, and felt a tickle of resentment. He must think I'm really inept, I told myself, to go explaining something like that.

But the feeling in my belly was no longer anything like pleasure. The tiniest bit of pee leaked from me, and I felt it blot into my underwear. I groped for him, and tried to hang onto him, drag him away.

He cringed just far enough to avoid me.

I sensed his laughter. His voice was a whisper, but it was a statement that canceled every thought in my mind. "I'll be back in ten seconds."

Come away with me, my soul called, as though he were already someone who could be reached only by prayer. Please, Jared.

He was gone.

I had always known he was like no one else. But now I understood what a rare creature he was. Jared could feel no doubt, and no fear. He was like no other human being.

And he had left, to escape from the ordinary company of a person like me. I felt what Jared must see in me: how common I was, how unsure of myself.

I should have held him, wrestled him, made a noise to force Jared out of the house. Even now I could call out, and wake up the sleeping strangers.

There was a whisper of footfall on the stairs, a sound I sensed more than heard. There was, more than that, a silence that spilled upward, into the second floor, a nonsound that I knew was Jared's presence.

I held my breath for a moment, imagining—*knowing*—

that he must be in the bedroom now, must be creeping toward the dresser with its dimly lit personal treasures.

I huddled, my heart beating so hard, each beat rocked my body, my throat so constricted I nearly could not breathe.

It ended quickly.

Brakes moaned outside, and a car door made a metallic cough as it was flung open. There were two cars, and steps on the pavement—crisp, hard noises that were at the very edge of my hearing.

Yet a third car sighed into place somewhere in the street, beyond and far away and yet right there, right inside me, each quick footfall, each creak of clothes or leather, sounds not heard so much as felt, like the mutterings of my own body, the clicks and whispers of my insides.

The fanged voice in me said: let's see you turn invisible now.

Tires crackled on the asphalt, and a car jockeyed to a new place in the night, perhaps to block the street, and as it worked into the position a light flashed red, splashes of vermilion blinking off and on.

The scarlet warning flashes lasted for only a few heartbeats, and then someone, an unseen hand, snapped it off.

But the blunder had been made.

Wooden floors made the softest click. Jared was on the stairs. I straightened, lips parted, screaming in my mind: *run!*

But Jared was there in the hall, his silhouette blocking sight of the little red star for an instant. The sight of him spun me, freed me to escape because I knew he was right there, behind me as I ran. I skittered briefly on the waxed floor, plunged into the laundry room, and snaked my way through the window.

I did not fall. I clung, gasping, to the sill.

A flashlight worked the dark. The beam swung toward me and missed. It pooled on the brilliant blades of grass, then swung from tight circle to oblong. It pulled back toward me where I squirmed, dangling from the window.

I fell.

What you have to do, Jared had said, is roll, lowering your shoulder, tumbling into the fall. That way you can't get hurt. I have injured myself before. I lost time as a sophomore, having to study at home because I stepped funny on second base.

My mouth filled with warm water. I was all over the grass, one arm far away, by the fence, the other hand squashing an ice plant. My skull was in fragments, all wet and leaking, the crushed bits of it rasping as I jerked my head.

Jerked, and then woke.

I plunged upward, onto my feet, and staggered. I tasted blood, and ran a ragged, drunken course to the back fence, barely aware of what my legs and arms were doing as they fought the back fence, punched it, kicked it, found some purchase in a knothole, a splintery grip at the top edge.

I windmilled over the top of the fence, and half stumbled to the gritty pavement. I lunged onward through the dark, and then I saw it.

It was the distinctive shape of a police car, that brute-vehicle menace that means: power.

I stopped myself, bent double, and knelt. The ground

swung back and forth around me. Nausea flashed on and off.

Jared was nowhere.

I had left him behind.

I put my hands to my hair, feeling above my ear for the stuff that had leaked from inside my head. It was wet and gluey. My fingers moved gingerly, and I knew that a brain infection was what I deserved for abandoning my friend.

Back. I have to go back.

I stood up slowly. My hand felt for support, and found a cinderblock wall. I was going to throw up, and then, just as surely, I wasn't.

I knew where I had to go.

I sprinted back toward the fence, one of my knees so weak I ran with a crazy limp. But I was fast.

Until I realized that my body had grown heavy. I was slow and fighting something. I was struggling to overcome a strange, ungainly weight. I was struggling against a shadow that clung.

It was a human being.

My adversary's grip was on my shoulder, and pulling me back by one arm.

I went down.

Caught.

———

12

So this is what happens.

The law had me, the law and all it involved, things I could imagine only as blank-faced authority, loveless and without mercy. I saw it now. How could I have forgotten? The gray world, adult and without life, was always going to catch me. It catches everyone.

There was the splash of a thought, a pain more than a memory: my parents. This will be an ugly surprise for them.

I tried to stir, and I was, to my amazement, able to move my arms and legs. The arms that held me were not strong at all, not nearly as strong as I was. They trembled.

He was laughing.

"You ran like a crab, Stanley."

I tossed myself free and stood. I spat blood, panting.

"Like a crab," he said. "All bent over."

"What happened to you?" I asked before I was aware of being able to speak.

His foot splashed a puddle. He was gone, and I followed, over another fence, and across a pile of rattling boards, dim and warped in the darkness. A dog was upon us, wagging its tail and growling, exposing its teeth and leaping around us, wanting to kill us and play with us at the same time.

Jared spoke to it, ran a hand over its back. The dog continued to growl, but pranced away as we flung ourselves over a gate and out across another dew-slick lawn.

He ran much better than I did. My own legs had grown new joints, which swiveled as I ran. There was a numbness in my skull that would, I knew from experience, ripen into pain very soon.

Jared vanished through a tangle of fennel, down into a culvert beside an electricity substation surrounded by a chain-link fence with barely visible HIGH VOLTAGE signs. The equipment within made a quiet sound, a sneaky, galactic hum.

I crouched, sweating and cold. Jared shook out a cigarette and I accepted it. We shared, for a moment, that almost sexy leaning-together over a match. He shook it out, and smoked with the glowing end cupped inward, toward his palm, a method I copied at once.

Would I throw up?

He looked away, distracted. From far off there came the mutter of a cop radio. The stabs of static drifted, and faded away.

I was trembling, queasy, and the chain-link fence spun up and down, and then from side to side. Closing my eyes made it worse. The earth swung away from beneath me.

"I walked out the back door," said Jared. "Unhooked the chain. I took my time."

I bit my knuckle. I had abandoned him.

"It was easy," he said. Then, as though I had expressed disbelief, "It really was."

Of course. Ash trembled off the end of my cigarette. It had been entirely easy.

For him.

The stalks of the fennel around us, and the old, cast-off stalks we were sitting on, gave off a fragance. The air smelled of licorice and tobacco. One of the white metal signs on the chain-link read PELIGROSA. There was a picture of lightning striking a human figure. The fence was old, a black net made of metal, and sloppy rolls of barbed wire festooned the top rail.

"And I brought a really rare prize," he continued. "It's something pretty unusual. Which I give to you."

He tossed me something warm and round. I handled it for a moment, feeling the lightweight lump, fibrous and foreign in the bad light. Then I let it drop. I didn't want to touch this stolen object. It was something medical, I sensed, something repulsive out of a person's body, a hairball or a weird tumor.

He drew on his cigarette and laughed. "You wear them," he said, "on your feet."

I drew the smoke in all the way, so deep it burned, and let it out, pushing the entire shame out of my lungs until my breath came out clear, empty, and clean. "I'll do it right," I said in a little, dry voice.

He smoked.

"Next time," I said clearly, "I'll do it right."

"You'll have a chance. There's something I didn't tell you."

I let the smoke out in twin streams through my nostrils. The smoke was having an effect on me, making me feel separate from my arms and legs, and the nausea was completely dead. Jared leaned forward, waiting for me to ask. So I gestured with the glowing cigarette: what?

"They weren't home."

I WOKE FEELING DEAD.

I did not move for a while, and when I began to find my way up, away from the pillow, I sat up quickly, clutching the sheets to my throat.

The matter in my head had leaked out onto the pillowcase.

There was not much of it, but there was a definite dark crushed substance, several fragments of it. I recognized it very slowly as snail shell.

I washed the pillowcase out very carefully in the bathroom sink, and then I washed my hair under the shower, telling myself: my parents won't know.

Nobody will know anything.

13

I COULDN'T LEAN MY HEAD against my hand because my cranium was sore there. I tried slumping way back and down, but the chair met the back of my skull and that hurt, too. So I sat up straight.

"They charged into cannon fire. Eyes scalded, blinded by the smoke. Some of them permanently deafened by the noise. Deaf for the rest of their lives from that day." Mr. Milliken paced up and down. He glanced at me, and I must have smiled or looked pleasant because he gave a quick little smile himself.

"A cannonball didn't blow up," announced Mr. Milliken. "It didn't explode and make a nice fountain of dirt, like you see in movies. Cannonballs took off arms. Legs. Heads."

I was not sure, exactly, how pain medications are supposed to work. Is it something they do at the synapse? Do they keep neurons from firing?

The pills were having no effect at all, or only a little. I could move my neck.

I was aware of Sky, rows away from me. When she bent to make a note in her three-ring, when she ran the point of the pencil back through her long hair, I knew it, even if I wasn't looking.

Mr. Milliken was, as usual, trying to sell us history by making it into something you could see on a tabloid: ANCIENT WEAPONS BLOW OFF ARMS AND LEGS. SEVERED HEAD FLIES THROUGH AIR LOOKING AND THINKING.

It had been Mr. Milliken's contention one day, in an attempt to stir his class awake, that a severed head could see and remember, and even gaze out in wonderment at its new condition. The Revolutionary War, under discussion, had segued into the French Revolution and the guillotine. Just as now the Civil War was about to drift into the Gatling gun. We were never going to make it to the H-bomb.

47

I was a mess from the night before. Not a wreck; I can take punishment. My neck was stiff and I had the very slightest double vision. My mother's medicine cabinet had furnished some Tylenol and some pills that I supposed were for menstrual cramps. I had taken them, too.

To encourage Mr. Milliken, I leaned forward and drew a small explosion next to the pink line that marked the margin. I wanted him to think I was taking notes. I needed the distraction. I was seared inside with my new understanding: I was trapped.

It was so painful that I tried to edge away from the word.

But I could hear Jared's laugh, kind and mocking at once. He knew, and I knew, the truth. I was a coward until I played the game again.

"Chain shot!" Mr. Milliken nearly shouted, desperate to keep our attention. "Howling, twisting chains cutting men in two."

The board read: *Civil War. Causes. Armaments.* But what swept Mr. Milliken was the great hunger to have all of us quiet. And more than that. He wanted us to care. "Grapeshot," he said, getting hoarse. "Point-blank. Bodies atomized."

The bell rang, and Mr. Milliken slumped on his podium. His freckled face was flushed, and I could tell by the way he did not meet our eyes that he was fatigued by his performance, and at the same time sure that it was wasted on television-dazed cattle. I already understood that Mr. Milliken did not relish the destructive details he recounted. He found them of some interest, but he believed that only gore could keep the attention of his class.

"Nice lecture," I said as I passed, and Mr. Milliken gave me a careful look, wary that I was being sarcastic, hopeful that I was being sincere. "It was no joke," he said, meaning his lecture or the Civil War. "I don't know if it was ignorance or courage that made them go through it."

He said this quietly, half to me, but, so not to embarrass either of us if I didn't give a damn, half to the podium, a maple-stained plinth made of plywood.

Then he realized that he was going to be late for Driver's Education, his next class and mine. I could tell by the way he started bubbling-in spaces in his roll book that he had forgotten to post the absences.

I was stalling, lingering, hoping to fall in with Sky as she left the class. But she was already out the door, having, I realized too late, waved with her fingers, a casual, careless little hello wave.

Such waves are friendly, but not intimate at all—not even a little. I would need a plan, something ambitious.

She *was* smiling, I consoled myself. It was a genuine smile, with that sideways look she has. I was warmer inside considering that.

"I have made a decision," said Mr. Milliken.

He stuffed papers into a scuffed black briefcase, a big worn leather thing like something Drama could borrow for *Death of a Salesman*. He fell into stride with me, both of us shouldering through the crowded halls.

There was something sincere about Mr. Milliken, eager and honest, even though he was sick of his job. I did not attempt to flee him, even when he said, "I picked you."

We passed Sky's locker, but she was not there. I was too warm, the air was too close, and I thought I must have misheard him.

"You," he repeated, hollering over the rumble of arguments, laughter, and the whack of locker doors thrown shut.

My expression must have asked: for what? But I had already guessed.

He laughed. He actually laughed, and I could tell that he was not a teacher now so much as an adult feeling good for just a passing moment. "It's a key moment," he said. "We're going to die together."

14

DRIVER'S ED HAD BOASTED several driving simulators, which I had never had a chance to use because they had been stolen the summer before. Instead, we had been taking quizzes on the California State Vehicle Code and watching films produced by the Highway Patrol, which included endless footage of car wrecks. Drivers in clothes that looked awkwardly out of style and pedestrians looking somehow historical lay bloody beside mammoth, by now obsolete, ambulances. The dated quality of the films made them less real, of course, but it also made them weigh in with a heavy, hard-to-shake-off message: dead then, dead now.

Sometimes someone would have trouble figuring out what a particularly awful burn victim was supposed to be; one or two looked like charred birds. "What was that?" I would hear whispered, or not whispered, but no one would respond. I think we were most of all embarrassed by all these victims. We had to look, but we hated it and liked it at the same time.

But the cars had arrived at last, new Chevrolets of a sort no one ever drove in Oakland, four-door cars that seemed destined to belong to chemistry teachers and Baptist ministers, solid, dull people in a safe place like Kansas or Iowa. These cars all sported a yellow triangle of wood, like the triangle you use to set up the balls in a pool game, but bigger and emblazoned: STUDENT DRIVER.

Mr. Milliken was going driving with me. He got paid extra for teaching driving, padding his wallet with a little excitement.

I only wanted to zombie my way through the day. This was not the time to introduce my practically auto-virgin self behind the wheel.

But he stood with a clipboard beside the Chevrolet. He waited at the passenger's side while I fumbled with the car door. Two girls I knew only a little, Asian girls who regarded me with both charm and indifference, Dung and Tina, sat in the backseat, and I thought they might be pouting a little at having to wait.

51

"Mr. Milliken thinks I'm going to kill us all," I said.

Tina chewed gum at me.

"I wouldn't have even mentioned the word *death* if I thought there was any danger," said Mr. Milliken.

Dung was from Vietnam. She was pretty, and little, so little you had to keep looking at her. She had the fine features and delicate jawline I associate with pictures of Egyptian mummies.

Tina was rough, gum-popping, and bored with me, with cars, with air. Although she had the crisp English of a gangster in an old movie, her native language was Mien. Tina heard my offer and curled a lip. "Doesn't matter," she said.

Dung laughed. No, no, I should go first. But she sidled her way into the front seat ahead of me.

"A drive to the park," said Mr. Milliken, in the artificially cheerful tone of the narrator in a travel film.

Tina blew bubbles beside me in the back seat. Each big bubble grew huge, then grew lopsided, then collapsed and withered. She unpeeled it from her face each time and stuffed it back in.

"We should go over to San Francisco," said Tina. "Have some fun."

Dung drove looking up and over the steering wheel, as though she could barely see out through the windshield.

"Looking good," said Mr. Milliken.

We drove up Park Boulevard and then really started to drive, picking up speed as Dung felt the command of the wheel and the accelerator suddenly hers.

"Gotta watch that limit," said Mr. Milliken, pumping the brake of his controls. He had a gas pedal and a brake but no steering wheel.

I did not look off to our left, where the neighborhood of large, spacious houses began. I knew the house with green shutters was there, beyond sight, just as I knew I would have to visit it again.

When it was Tina's turn, we were on Snake Road. She blew a bubble, jerked the car out of park, and whipped us up the two-lane road.

At Redwood Park, after Tina had negotiated the twists of the road with disdain, using two hands only at Mr. Milliken's prompting, it was my turn.

"Into the Valley of Death," said Mr. Milliken.

I had driven once before—my father's Honda, which, since it is a stick shift, hopped like a rabbit every time I popped the clutch. I am a fairly athletic person, used to being able to come up with the ball one way or another, but I had decided to wait on driving until I got a car I could handle.

I could tell Dung and Tina were both relieved that they had made it this far, and were ready to be entertained by whatever blunders I might make.

"What kind of bombs were they?" I said, hoping to distract my nerves and Mr. Milliken's humor with a little history. "The ones that burst in midair? You know—in the song."

"Not car bombs," he said.

The shift was a metal T, and when the transmission slipped from park into reverse, you could feel the gears in there, under there, beyond us, finding what it was I had commanded. I had that wonder I had known as a very little boy watching a helicopter: machine.

"This is boring," said Tina.

The car backed, gravel crackling. I worked the wheel around and found drive. I tested the accelerator, which generated more noise than movement. I tested the brake, and the slight forward movement stopped.

I turned my head to acknowledge Mr. Milliken, feeling cheerful, nervous. Little Dung made the tiniest noise clearing her throat.

The car surmounted a hump at the ridge of the parking lot, and the road was littered with scraps of eucalyptus, tree trash all over the place. The air smelled wonderful. I found the lane with the car, and let the car's momentum take one curve after another, downhill and easy.

"Too slow," said Tina.

THAT NIGHT I SAT UP STRAIGHT, and put my hand out into the dark.

I whispered Jared's name, and listened. It would be just like him to steal into my own room as I slept, right into my bedroom, just to prove that he could do it.

But there was no sound, or only the normal sounds of the trees in the backyard making a fine, soft breathing noise in the wind.

———

15

"I THINK I MADE A MISTAKE, Stanley."

I did not respond. I was waiting for Sky, and felt both confined and honored to be in the garage. "Dad told me so. He said, 'Two hundred and twelve thousand' and laughed."

Tu leaned over the engine of his car. He held a wrench, which made a pleasing ratcheting sound as he spun it around and around. "God damn," he said, seriously and without sounding angry, the two words separate and careful. "Too many miles."

Perhaps he misunderstood my lack of response as a macho no-comment way of agreeing with him. It was true that the afterglow of my student driving was still with me. It takes more than a few hours for something like that to wear off. But I could not trick myself into believing that I had cars figured out.

"Bad carburetor," said Tu. "Bad everything."

"There must be something good about it," I offered.

"What do you think?" asked Tu, almost challengingly. He had, like his sister, a slight accent. His *t*'s sounded just slightly like *d*'s, and his words were delivered slowly, each syllable with weight.

I shook my head, meaning: I wouldn't know.

"A piece of junk." Tu grinned painfully, misunderstanding

my blank look for something more manly and more dignified.

He tossed the wrench, and it hit in a place on the work-bench padded with cloth so the tool made a soft thump. Tu spun the butterfly nut on top of the engine, and tossed it to me. My baseball reflexes snatched the little winged nut from the air before I could think.

Tu lifted away a big circular device, a car part grimy and gray, and set it aside.

We both looked into the exposed engine. Tu prodded a valve with his finger. The small trapdoor made the slightest squeak.

"I don't know anything," I said. "At all." My words were not the simple confession I intended. They were naked statements, and I hurried to add, "About cars."

Tu worked his fingers into a rag. "I think the car has a good heart."

"Cars are a little mysterious," I suggested cautiously.

He looked me in the eye. "Not so mysterious, Stanley."

I thought for a moment he was criticizing me.

"Sky has volleyball practice," he said, working a flap in the engine that was uneasily bright amidst the grime of the rest of the machine.

I wanted to say: I know. I wanted to clear my throat and say something about how good she was at sports. We both knew she was late.

"She doesn't understand," said Tu. "About things. She doesn't understand the way guys think. Girls are different. They think about other things."

"I like Sky," I began.

Tu looked at me and shook his head, leaning toward me. He was a senior and only a year older than I was, but there was something about his bearing that gave him dignity. "You don't know Sky very well yet," he said.

The "yet" sounded promising, I thought. Or hoped.

"You should know a couple of things," he said.

My expression must have silenced him, or perhaps it was the weight of what he had to say. He bit his lip for a moment. "Sky knows some people."

This was hardly news, but I went dry inside.

He gestured with a hand, perhaps missing the wrench to play with. "A lot of people at our church."

He wiped his hands on his jeans. "And she has a boyfriend already, Stanley. A big boyfriend. Goes to Hoover."

I wanted to lean against something.

"I like him okay," Tu said. "But I don't really like him all that much."

My voice was a thin little noise, barely human. "What does Sky think of him?"

Tu leaned against the car and gazed at the engine. "I think she likes him, Stanley."

The sunlight through the open garage door was an ugly bleached yellow, hard on the eyes.

Tu lurched around the car and flung himself into the front seat. The big old Ford slumped to one side with his weight. "Okay," he called, "open that valve. Like I was doing. That little valve."

I moved in small jerks, thinking: you don't have to explain which valve. I'm not a total idiot. I was also thinking what a loud voice Tu had, and how he really ought to work on keeping it down so it wouldn't sound so annoying to people.

The engine made several distinct sets of squeaks as his foot depressed the accelerator before he turned the starter. The absence of engine rumble made the smaller hinges and connections of the car click and squeak.

I blocked out the garage for a moment, thinking of those other car sounds I had heard in the house with green shutters. Those other little car sounds, those hushes and thuds. My chest went tight and I felt weak at the memory, which was not a memory at all but a physical and present fact, like my skin or my bones. I felt dizzy.

The blast of the engine made me jump back. The big machine chattered, and was powerful, even dangerous, the fan blade spinning so fast it was a blur. Then the engine whirred into silence.

"Use a tool or something, Stanley," said Tu from inside the car. "Hold it open. The car needs lots of air."

I had to force my attention into the engine and poke the screwdriver where it belonged, holding open the trapdoor valve as Tu clicked the ignition. The car made that robot laugh old cars make when they have trouble starting. And then the engine caught, rumbled, and Tu pumped the roar, played it, until the big car idled.

"We're doing okay," called Tu. "We got power after all, Stanley," he said. I smiled at him through the dust of the windshield, as exhaust crept forward from the rear of the garage. Power after all. The phrase seemed political, or like something from an ad, and Tu laughed, aware that he had been quoting something, or misquoting.

I thought: tell Tu. Tell Tu all about Jared and the game.

I needed to talk to him, and hear what he would say.

I needed to tell someone.

Tu climbed out of the car, and the car settled back again. There was satisfaction on his face as he held out his hand so I could drop the butterfly nut into the creases of his palm.

Tu slammed the hood by lifting it a little higher to disengage the hinge and then throwing the hood down hard, back where it belonged.

We both coughed against the exhaust, and Tu smiled. "You want to drive?"

I shrank. I began to say that I didn't know how to drive, that I had missed Driver's Ed as a sophomore because of my ligament, that I didn't even have a learner's permit. And just as quickly I thought, sure. Why not?

But Tu was already in the front seat, and the car was rolling, and as we made our way down the driveway, Sky stopped at the sidewalk, gazing at us with her head held slightly back, an empress enjoying the sport of her subjects, her eyes nearly closed, telling her brother: so you got it moving.

It caught me, how well they knew each other.

"Hey," Tu called, "get in the car. We're going for a ride."

And the way he said it made it sound like we were going to go for a drive into the afternoon sky, over the sea.

"This is no car," she said scornfully, and more than that, lovingly.

We drove to the intersection by the video store, and the big white car stuttered and rolled silent. Tu leaned his head on the steering wheel.

"It's okay," said Sky from the backseat.

A car behind us honked, and Sky turned back and called out so clearly I knew the driver could hear, "Our car is broken. Don't you have any sense?"

The car honked again, belligerently, and then the tires squealed and the car passed us.

Sky put her hand on my shoulder. "Come on, Stanley," she said, her breath in my ear, her hair tickling my neck. "Let's push."

16

MY MOTHER HAD A BLACK CARRY-ON over her shoulder. It was leather, the shiny, soft leather that makes a silky noise when it moves.

She was slipping a map into a side pocket. "Don't put so much salt on the popcorn," she said. "And if you use the microwave popcorn, make sure you open the packet away from your eyes. You might get blinded by the steam."

I was in my dad's chair, looking, as he often looked, at the blank television screen.

"Wait a minute," she said. "I thought for a second there was another person in the room, someone with ears who spoke English."

"Okay," I said.

"Christ."

The television screen was a peculiar color when you really took a moment to look at it. It was gray-green, a flat, empty green like nothing alive.

As so often before, the words came before I could stop them. "You feel guilty," I said.

She tugged at a zipper, and did not respond.

"You feel bad," I continued, hating to hear myself talk. "You worry about me eating enough fiber because you're running away all the time."

She let her black bag drop. "This is very interesting, one minute before my cab gets here."

"Never mind."

"Your basic form of conversation is sneaky, you realize that? You think communication is a long-running argument. You save up wise things to say. Reality as a sort of baseball game. You score points."

"Runs." I clamped my teeth on my tongue.

"I'm going to spend the night drinking coffee on the plane and finishing a report, have breakfast, look fresh and cute, and then I'm going to get on a plane and fly back here to an empty house."

I glanced at her, expecting an irritated, impatient person. Instead, I saw that she was near tears. "And you think you're so smart," she said, her voice soft and cutting. "Completely

61

disengaged. Just a passenger on this trip. You have nothing to do with anything."

I ached. I wanted to put my arms around her. I wanted to hide. "I'm sorry," I said, lips numb, my voice a rasp. I wanted to add a dozen other questions, but I gripped the arms of the chair. There was a honk outside.

"Sorry," she echoed, and I could sense her measuring me, wanting me to be a different sort of son, wanting her life to be something it wasn't.

She moved fast. She flung the carry-on over her shoulder, and only looked back from the door. "It's a disaster," she said, so calmly that it made her statement into a statement of fact, ugly and beyond dispute. "A complete disaster."

And she was gone, just like that, her eyes glittering with things she wanted to say, or was afraid to say, and I sat there, my words drying up, gazing after the closing door.

I MADE A POINT OF EATING with my father that night, an uncommon event. We had Mrs. Paul's clam crisps and a spinach soufflé in a plastic bag that looked like a green rock until you cooked it. I asked how things were going at the foundry, hoping to hear about molten steel and gigantic drop forges slamming out axles or exhaust manifolds.

"Our dental plan has fled the country," said my father.

He said this with just the slightest wry tone, so I knew I was supposed to ask for more information. I was slow that night.

"I have spent the afternoon talking to the world's rudest dental receptionists, those sweet ladies who reassure you when you lose a filling." He put down his fork. "I knew there was trouble," he said, "when Macroplan wouldn't answer the phone for two months." He let air out through his teeth. "I should have played it differently. Finessed it somehow."

I got ready to ask him to tell me all about it, but when I looked at him, I really studied him. He was tired, dark smudges under his eyes, and he hadn't shaved very well that morning. There was a little stand of whiskers under one nostril. He had a handsome, craggy face, and looked exactly like what he was—a smart man with many worries. He was drained, and not just from recent struggles. He was getting used up.

"You know what life comes down to," he said with a little smile. It wasn't a question. It was one of those topic sentences my father liked to use in conversation: "you know what really pisses me off" or "you know what the problem with unemployment insurance is."

I gave him a look of interest, a hopeful smile.

"A good filing system." He laughed, an ironic sort of laughter I did not feel invited to join. "Isn't that depressing?"

I made a little questioning sound.

"Depressing because you expect life is a question of courage or brains or love or something. But the guy who knows where he put things, where the money is, where the facts are, and who can put his hands on the hot numbers the quickest is the winner. It wins wars. It wins hearts and lives.

It cures the halt and the lame. Not genius. Not the tireless, merciful soul. Those are nothing compared with a good information retrieval system."

He chewed, and I said: "Mother isn't happy."

His answer was quick. "Happy," both ironic and a little sad. He thought for a while. "That's my point."

He regarded me. "She's in Boston," he said, and I wanted to say that she was nowhere at all, really. She was in flight, finishing a report, but then it stung me: he didn't really know where she was, he was guessing, hoping that I knew. She hadn't told him.

After a long while, he said, "We may not make it."

My throat constricted and I stopped chewing. I had tears, blinding, quick tears, and I looked away so he wouldn't see.

His hand was on mine. "I shouldn't have said that. It's going to be fine, Stan. Don't worry."

I nodded, even tried to look a little tough. Sure. No problem.

I had irritated my mother beyond exasperation; I knew that. I suspected, too, that my father was weary at least in part because of me. A dental plan doesn't humble a man like my father. Without me, he could have taken a leave from his job, maybe, or quit it and found another. He could have done romantic things with my mother, bought her flowers and taken her away for weekends in Carmel.

But it wasn't fair to blame me. It wasn't fair. They couldn't count on me to hold things together for them. It wasn't right.

"You're okay, Stan? Really?"

I was okay. I was dead inside, but that seemed just about

normal for this time and place. It was one of life's IQ tests. If you felt wonderful you were stupid.

It was obvious that Jared was right. I could hear Jared's voice, sense his laughter. Don't waste your time trying to help these botched people.

Or, sure, you care about them. That's natural. They're your parents.

But there is only one way to feel alive.

17

A WHITE SHAPE BROKE from the tangle of geraniums, and half hopped to where Sky sat.

She caressed the large white cat, a creature who leaned into her and purred. The cat had strong-looking hind legs, and a single large front paw. Where the other forepaw belonged was nothing. Not a stump, not a scar.

"A dog bit him," she said.

This news silenced me. I stopped to caress the cat, too, and for a moment took pleasure in the fact that we were both touching the same living creature.

It was two days after I had helped push the big Ford back to the driveway. The car was there now, chocks behind the wheels to keep it from rolling, Tu bent over the engine. I had not seen Jared since the terrible night. Mrs. Trent had said he had a virus.

I had to talk to Jared. I had something to tell him.

"A German shepherd," said Sky. "The cat was bloody all over. I tied a tourniquet."

"You saved his life."

She rubbed the cat one way and another. The cat spasmed, purring, hunching. "He's a good cat."

"What's his name?"

"This isn't our cat. He is his own cat. No name."

"He likes you."

"He remembers me," said Sky. She looked up at me. "I know you used to pass by me and not know what to say."

I wanted to say something smart but couldn't think.

"And then you had your big chance with that guy on the football field."

"You needed some help."

"He wasn't so strong." She thought, and added, "That was a kind thing to do," then looked away. "I was a little surprised."

"Why were you surprised?" I said, more sharply than I wanted.

She tilted her head and did not answer, smiling at her own secret. "You try so hard, Stanley."

I bridled. "I do more than try." I hated my snippy tone, but it was really more than I could stand.

"I have offended Stanley," said Sky to the cat. "Now he will never like me."

"Oh, I'll like you," I said, and I hated the tone of my

66

voice. I said it as though regretting it. I was doing everything wrong. Being close to her made me an idiot. I blundered further, aghast at my words. "Tu says you have a boyfriend."

She gave a sideways look, her head tilted back, regal and very slightly offended. Her long black hair, full and high-lighted with a burnish of mahogany, flowed about her, and her dark eyes took me in, weighed me, held me. "What does Tu say?"

"He says there's someone else you know."

"I know many people, Stanley." She was solemn, but she was something else, too. Was she also teasing me, just a little? I tingled inside at the thought. It was an almost pleasant feeling.

"Tu likes you," she added.

"I don't know anything about cars," I said, wondering why I insisted on making such a baldly honest statement.

She looked at me sideways again. She was smiling, in-wardly, and her eyes were narrow and searching my own eyes. "I think you know some things," she said.

"I like history," I said, chattering on like someone who has taken sodium pentothal and absolutely has to blab the truth. "It would be wonderful to be a historian. To go back and figure out how things were and tell people about it."

"I thought you were very different."

That shut me up.

"I thought you were going to be in trouble."

"How?"

"With Jared."

"I hardly know Jared."

This first lie, out so quick, surprised me, and I sank back, away from what I had said, actually leaning back against the step. The concrete ledge dug into my backbone. A sow bug, curled up into a little seed, rolled in place beside my elbow. I had just now nearly crushed it.

"I used to know him," I added, for the sake of plausibility, and also because I knew she had seen the two of us together. To salvage some self-respect, I continued, "He's really an interesting guy."

The cat purred under her hand. "You should meet my father," she said.

I looked out at the front yard, the big palm tree with its huge, dropped feathers and old date pits, the quiet street. A pigeon clapped through the air. I could see that talking with Sky was going to be an unusual experience. She didn't indulge in the paragraphs that come between the title and the conclusion.

"He saw you," she added. "When you were here, pushing the car."

I helped the sow bug back to the edge of the steps and off into the geraniums.

"He wants to meet everyone," she said. I knew she meant everyone Sky was involved with. Did that mean, I wondered, that I was involved with her? But it was easy to imagine Mr. Tagaloa: gigantic, with dark, intelligent eyes. The sort of grown man who sees into someone like me, and knows. I had seen him only once or twice, a large man driving a copper-brown van picking up Sky after school.

"But I have to think first." She looked away. I had always wanted to talk with Sky, as I was now, but I had not anticipated her turns of thought. She leaned toward me, her eyes on mine, and said, "We have skunks."

"Aren't they kind of a nuisance?" When she didn't respond, I added, "They eat garbage, don't they?"

"Sometimes. I used to see their footprints around the garbage cans. I feed them."

I took a breath, gazed at the palm tree, and said, "They must like you."

She was laughing then, her eyes nearly vanished, a large, quiet laugh, so much like Jared's way of laughing that I twitched and fell very still. "You think I'm crazy."

"No." I said that very quickly.

"You think I'm lying, don't you, Stanley?"

"Why would you lie? It's nothing to brag about." I clenched my fists. Talking with her was a disaster.

"My father will like talking to you, Stanley. He knows a lot." She watched her brother open the car door and lie down on the front seat, his legs sticking out into the sunlight.

"Come over on Saturday," she said without looking at me. "My father will be ending a plague. At least, that's the way he looks at it."

The Biblical turn of her phrase, and the fact that it didn't really make any sense, stopped me.

She laughed. "Not you," she said. "You aren't a plague."

Then she added, enjoying, I think, the fact that I didn't quite understand her, "I don't like killing."

69

18

THE GRAY WATER SHIFTED and surged around a man who swam in a circle, dog-paddling.

He splashed in a bewildered panic. Then he found it.

The floating object tossed in the water. It seemed to seek him. The severed leg floated toward his hand, bobbing, as another crocodile plunged into the water, and the beast that had taken his leg returned, torpedoing through the current to the man's splashes.

Jared switched it off. The screen went blank.

"You always wonder why the cameraman doesn't do something," I said after a while.

Jared was red-eyed, and my homework papers were scattered at his feet. "No," he said. "I don't wonder."

He wore a very old T-shirt featuring Fred Flintstone on a surfboard. Fred Flinstone was faded, and there were little holes worn in the fabric of the shirt. Sometimes Jared bought old clothes at Goodwill and wore them just to communicate something.

He was smoking yet another cigarette. Beside him, the ashtray on the pile of magazines held cigarette butts, charred seeds, and the remnants of stems.

On other evenings, Jared watched the death tape with interest. It was a collection of actual deaths, beheadings, firing squads, and in the one sequence that I hated most of all, the bewildered man who lost his leg to a crocodile.

Tonight Jared leaned on his elbow and made no move to turn on the screen, although the VCR was still running, and the tape must have reached the electrocution by now.

The marijuana taste was in my mouth, sticky and weedy, and my eyes burned from the smoke. I hadn't smoked very much, just enough to be polite—I had to finish my homework. The lampshade was turned to the wall, spilling an oblong of light behind Jared.

His mother had ushered me up the stairs, saying that she hoped I'd get him to feel better. There was a dinner party in progress, long white candles and long, narrow candle flames reflected off black bottles of wine.

"If you get shot, you have time to get downstairs," said Jared.

I laced my fingers together.

"Just a little nightstand gun." His nostrils flared with a yawn. "No kind of stopping power."

"I don't know what kind of gun it was. I never saw it."

"Maybe there wasn't a gun at all."

"I think there was."

"You probably imagined it." He said this almost sadly.

"Maybe he went and bought a gun, to go with his security system."

Jared shrugged. "I hope so."

His words made me turn slightly in my chair, so I did not face him so squarely. "I'm not going."

These words shocked me. I had no idea where they came

from. I was almost able to convince myself that I hadn't spoken them, except for Jared's response.

He half smiled, brushing an ash off his T-shirt without looking. "You have to."

"I'm quitting the game."

He closed his eyes briefly in his silent laugh. "You can't quit."

"I can't do it anymore."

He pulled hard on his cigarette, then lowered his chin to his chest. "I won't let you quit."

I made a breathy exclamation, a whispered syllable of frustration.

"I want to get him to use his gun," he said. "I want to risk everything, right up to the edge."

I said something I had been thinking about for a long time. Not the words so much, but the thought. "It's sick."

"What?" His voice was hard, even though quiet. I knew he had heard me quite well.

I didn't say anything else.

"You think this is just a game," said Jared. "You think it's like some kind of Monopoly you can pick up and put down when it bores you."

I shook my head, and did not meet his eyes.

"It's sick," he mocked. He folded his hands and looked nearly kind. "You're so ordinary, Stanley. You could change, you know. You don't have to be one of these dull people."

Why I had tears just then I did not know. I looked away and cleared my throat, blinking.

Perhaps the marijuana made the spill of light brighter, and

made the fibers of the carpet distinct, the thousands of un-noticed filaments bound together into a seamless mass.

"I know I owe you," I said. "I know I was a coward."

The ugly words made it hard for me to speak, to breathe.

"But I can't." I shook my head. I couldn't say any more for several heartbeats. I closed my eyes. "It's all over. I can't do it."

"You're going to try to go back," he said. "To your old, dead life."

I didn't answer. I had learned silence from my parents.

"But you can't," Jared said, calm, soft-voiced. "You can't walk away from feeling alive."

I knew he might be right.

19

THE LARGE MAN WAS SWEATING, uncoiling a hose and looking up into the tree. The hose was new, and it squeaked, the coiled circles wound into it not shaking out very well. The hose wriggled, a long, looping spiral.

The tree had a trunk about as big around as my leg. The branches were naked except for subtle black movement. What appeared to be leaves on the twigs and branches were slowly wriggling. The wriggling larvae had fed on all the foliage, and now the black, spiked grubs were starving, raining slowly onto the lawn.

His hand surrounded mine, but he kept his grip gentle.

Sky made the introduction, and then she vanished, leaving me in the backyard with her father.

"Baseball," he said.

I followed his thought after a pause. "A little." I didn't tell him that I had basically taken myself off the team in recent weeks.

He whipped the green hose, and far away a loop of it straightened out.

I had met Sky's mother a few times, a woman who, as far as I could tell, never spoke, a round, slow-moving woman in outsized T-shirts. Sky's father didn't talk much either. He twitched the hose and did not talk at all, and yet he was not ignoring me. His work was convivial, a sharing of his presence, the way some people might whistle or hum a song when someone is around even though they don't want to say anything.

I sat on a low wall made of bricks. The light was both bright and gray, and the bare tree was alive in places with caterpillars.

"I used to want to be an athlete," he said. The hose flicked again, the pulse traveling in a wave along the length of the green hose to where it screwed into the wall.

He turned his back to me, and I made out by his motions and the glimpses I caught that he was fastening a container of poison to the mouth of the hose.

He did not bother to glance over at me to see if I was paying attention. He was used to commanding people with his size, and as a result was friendly and full of confidence in himself. He drove a truck that delivered big bags of ready-popped popcorn to movie theaters.

"I worked all over," he said, scuffing his foot over some of the larvae. "I worked in Hollywood, delivering."

He looked at me as though he wanted to remember something he didn't like about me. "It's all fake," he said. "Those buildings. You know those buildings? Only half-buildings. You walk around them and they aren't there."

The poison container looked like a space gun worked by a lever. He sprayed poison all over the naked tree, and all over the black, still-crawling larvae, and the ones that weren't moving anymore, and all over the grass under the tree.

I moved back and sat on an overturned wheelbarrow so I wouldn't inhale the yellow poison, but he wasn't even wearing a respirator. "Chinese elm," he called. "Nothing but problems."

SKY WANTED TO KNOW what her father and I had talked about.

"It was pretty profound," I said.

"He's very serious."

We were both eating pattimelts on Piedmont Avenue. It was the first time we had ever eaten anything together, and I was eating very slowly.

She added, "He believes in me, Stanley."

75

She said this so solemnly that I needed to make a joke of some kind. "Is there some question? Do some people say you don't exist?"

Having said that, I didn't like the sound of it. Sky's family was not to be joked about.

Her eyes were downcast, and she was no longer eating. "He worries all the time."

"He looks calm."

"He's slow, but he's not calm, Stanley."

I ate the crust of my pattimelt, which was crunchy and flavored with cheesy grease.

"He remembers some stuff about you."

"I'm an all-right person." The statement sprang out of me, and I grabbed a paper napkin.

"But you remember when the school blew up."

This made me crumple my napkin into a wad. "That's ridiculous," I said, feeling small and futile.

The school had blown up before I had even gone there, before I was even a freshman. I had slept through it, but it blew out windows from Trestle Glen to Chinatown. Dozens of students had been questioned, past, present, and future high school students, and I had been dragged into the investigation because I used to smoke cigarettes behind the auto-shop building.

"He would hate it if I got in any kind of trouble, Stanley."

"Does knowing me automatically mean you're in trouble?" I really can't stand the way words spit out of me.

Sky took my hand from across the table and opened it up,

actually turned it over and parted my fingers with hers without looking at it, looking right into my eyes all the time.

"Tu likes you a lot," she said.

"But you don't," I heard myself say.

Sky doesn't strike poses, and she doesn't flirt. She considered my words. "I like you, too," she said.

I thought: *but*. She's going to say, "but . . ."

She didn't. She glanced down, and kept her hand where it was.

"Who is this other guy?" I said, and wanted to put my hands over my mouth.

She withdrew her hand. "He's not important."

But she said this regretfully, as though the other guy was a large, churchgoing, nonsmoking person her father adored.

Careful, I told myself.

Be very careful.

20

I SWUNG HARD, and missed.

The pitching machine was a gun, a cannon, and it fired so hard the pitches were streaks. The machine made a high, musical note, clicked, and then whipped another pitch to the back of the cage.

Afternoon: that second chance in the day, that chance to do something right.

I fouled one off, and the velocity spun the pitch up, into the sagging chain-link above. I didn't belong here anymore. But the other players let me take a turn, remembering the days when I used to belong there. Surely I would do so well this afternoon that the coach would see me and change his mind. Surely I had a right to a second chance. Everyone knew how hard I tried.

I wasn't doing too badly. Not well, but not a disaster, either. I loved the smell of grass under my cleats, the blades squashed and releasing that scent of newness. I knocked the damp earth out of my cleats. I had been wrong, I saw this now. I should have been here every afternoon, where I belonged.

Jared had dragged me away, convinced me that sports were for losers, and the best sport of all was his own secret game. He had been right. His sport was better, but I was happy to be back in this diminished—duller but more real, and safer— game.

The aluminum bat made that sour *boink*. The machine was set for eighty miles an hour and finally I was lining into the cage, making the steel poles hum. But too many of the pitches still kissed the bat and sprang upward, or spun at my feet.

The label on the bat said that it was made of aircraft-quality aluminum. The machine made that whine, that *tick*, and fired another ball out of its cannon. Eighty miles an hour. Fast, but not incredible.

Far away, Jared was sitting on the stands, a tiny figure. I

let the head of the bat drop to the dirt. I flexed my shoulders. Let him watch, I thought.

Let him sit there watching all he wants. I don't care anymore.

A ball hummed past me, unchallenged.

I opened my stance just a little, whipped my bat out to meet the cannon fire, and the next couple of pitches sang on a straight line.

Other players were waiting, and Tu was there, hands on his hips, too big for baseball, too easygoing to play any sport, but right where he belonged.

"Hit it with the bat, Stanley," called Tu, and none of the other players joined Tu in mocking me. They all understood that something had changed. I belonged, somehow, to Tu, and he had the right, in a subtle way that cost me no further effort, to tease me and at the same time would step in to protest any catcall from anyone else. "Hit the ball with the bat," he called.

The scuffed grass was covered with old baseballs, scratched, gouged. Too many of them lay behind me, untouched. The aluminum shaft had grown heavy, and my grip was clammy. I could feel the cigarettes, too, a tightness in my chest.

The coach arrived and hung on the chain-link the way a gibbon might, all arm and torso. I could tell by the way he watched that my swing was not what it should be.

I chopped at a pitch from the machine and the ball hummed, springing against the cage behind me.

I knew it was coming. "North," the coach said. "Get out

of there." But only after he had assessed me for a while, only after I had done well with some pitches, and not so well with others.

The coach and I walked into center field. Jared was a speck, unmoving. Looking on.

"Eat more, North. Jesus. You're getting skinnier every day."

I knew this was impossible, but I did not respond.

"It's not a matter of desire." He stuffed his hands into his pockets. He wouldn't look at me. "Desire is not the issue."

"A lot of shortstops aren't that muscular." I said this in a rotten little voice, with a catch in it. I gritted my teeth.

He looked at the ground, at the toe of his shoe. He looked out at the stands, where no one was sitting this late in the day, except for one distant figure. "Sure," he said at last, as though answering a question that had taken all his powers of memory and calculation. Then he looked at me. "Heart," he said. "You used to have a lot of that, before you got hurt. I think that torn ligament took more out of you than you think."

I stared at him, and had one of those moments when you really see someone. Beloved Coach Peoples, who had been on television when he retired, had left the baseball program with the best record in northern California. A combination of weird weather—it never rained this late in the spring—and beginner's bad luck had shaken this new coach, who was really a biology teacher.

He continued, "Some people, the first time they get hurt,

it really changes them. Sometimes the change isn't to the good."

He got extra money for standing here like this, but he had dandruff in his black hair and wrinkles under his eyes, just a little puffiness, as though he drank or couldn't sleep or both. Every racial and ethnic group on campus had wanted a coach who would represent their own group. Coach O'Brien was interesting ethnically, with a grandfather who had come from Mexico, but whose ancestors had emigrated from Ireland. He was sort of Hispanic and sort of Anglo, and had his own way of smiling down at the ground as though a grown man should be ashamed in front of his students.

His ballplayers almost never spoke to him directly. They liked him, in an unspoken way, but I think everyone was embarrassed for him because he wasn't Peoples.

I waited.

"I can't," said Coach O'Brien. "Bolt is too good. Shows up every day. And we've got Chau on the bench."

"I don't mind being a utility man," I said, although I felt my bones turn to iron. A voice in me said: Never. I'll never be third-string. I used to stop the ball with my eye socket, my teeth.

Coach O'Brien exhaled through his nostrils, a sad, quiet laugh. Someone had reset the machine and it was firing faster and harder, and a bat was snapping the ball straight ahead every time.

He laid a hand on my shoulder, and I knew that whatever he was saying, it wasn't yes.

21

I SLEPT BADLY, and could console myself only with the thought that Tu would tell Sky and their father that I was swinging the bat again.

My father's chair had been removed from the breakfast table, and was far off, by a wall. He had left, as usual, very early, the groan of the garage door briefly waking me in the dark. His dishes had long since been put into the dishwasher, but there was a faint outline of toast crumbs on his placemat.

"Was Boston okay?" I asked.

"Boston," she echoed, like the word was a bad joke. "I can't remember.

But her phone had been trilling, and her answering machine had a dozen calls on it whenever I happened to look. She was wearing a new bathrobe, with wide shoulders and a narrow waist. It was dark purple, and made a light, airy noise when she moved.

Maybe she was waiting for me to ask more questions, but I didn't.

I thought our conversation was over, and had stopped wishing that the news was on, when she said, "It was too much to expect you to be deaf and blind." She said this looking out of the window over the sink.

There was a cactus growing there, a green, spiky rock that just happened to be alive. It was not like either of my parents to have a plant. A gardener named Nolo came once a week to attack the hedge and mow the lawn, and when I was younger, I had thrilled at the chance to massacre some Bermuda hybrid with a Weed Whacker as Nolo took a cigarette break and looked on, chuckling.

We had always lived in this house, as far back as I could remember. But that wasn't true, I realized, sitting there shaping my toast into a modified jelly roll. There had been a long series of outside steps, sunny and made of crushed rock stuck together, slabs of glued-together gravel. This was all I could remember of another home, an apartment building. I had sat there, maybe three years old, as my mother ascended the steps, carrying groceries, the paper bag crackling, my mother laughing and nearly shrieking, a kind of jokey terror in her voice, because she thought my father was behind her, imitating a bear. He used to do that—pretend to be a big carnivore. But that had been a long time ago.

Besides, in this memory my father hadn't been chasing her after all, and she had stopped and looked back, waiting for him.

"I've been stalling," she said.

I pushed my plate away, unable to eat my toast and jelly.

"I'm not going to make it ugly for you and your father," she said. "That's how it is, I know that. You and your father."

I knew I was supposed to say something, but I shouldered silence toward her.

She was looking at me, really looking.

I looked back, and then my throat squeezed shut and I had to look away.

She turned and batted at the sink with a dishtowel, snapped at crumbs the way guys do in a locker room, a couple of snaps with the towel, as if for fun. Then she dropped the towel, and the terry cloth pooled at her feet.

Even when she left the kitchen, the length of towel kept the impression of her foot, arching over the place where it had been.

22

SKY WAS A STRONG WALKER.

"They'd be all gone, Stanley, if people still hunted them."

"Maybe not," I heard myself chirping. "There are still plenty of deer, and people hunt deer."

We were in Redwood Park, near where I had taken the wheel with Mr. Milliken for the first time. She had invited me to go exploring. I was panting to keep up, and nearly ran into her. She had stopped. "The passenger pigeon, Stanley. The American bison," she said in an even, low voice.

"Some people think people are a disease." I was delighted to agree, hating myself for speaking up so stupidly.

"I don't think we are a disease," she said. She hit me on the shoulder. "At least, not you, Stanley."

"I love the way you give compliments," I said.

She smiled. People smile all the time. But I had never seen anything like this. This was an expression that warmed and chilled me through my bones.

When we reached the top of the ridge, the hills fell away from us, tawny and shaggy-blue where there were trees. She unsnapped the binocular case, her hands careful, sure, and she pried the protective caps off the lenses.

"You can always see them here," she said.

I knew very little about birds, although I knew that the Romans had prized the eagle about as much as Americans did. I knew that Romans were superstitious about owls. I knew that falconry used to be an important sport.

But aside from history, I knew very little. The actual creatures were unknown to me. Sky, though, was comfortable with animals, and had even stopped to caress the muzzle of a horse tethered to a fence post while its rider wandered off somewhere. The horse had nickered at her as we walked on, already missing her.

Jared had this way with animals, too. A barking dog always fell silent or made its bark an I'm-only-kidding yelp when Jared strode by.

But Jared would never have scanned the scattered clouds like this, looking upward.

"They breed in the trees," she said. "In the tops of the redwoods."

It was all emptiness to me, but a good emptiness—promise. Then I saw one. Two, circling high up, tilting gracefully. I grabbed her arm.

Touching her like this stunned me. My hands leaped back. The strength of my feeling was surprising. I realized how little we had touched each other, and there I was, shaking her shoulder.

"Turkey vultures, Stanley."

My hands felt clumsy, foreign. I picked at a blister on my palm, a remnant of my batting practice.

"They are so pretty when you see them flying." She watched my vultures through the binoculars.

I thought that it was typical of me to pick a dead-meat-eater.

"They can float like that forever, on the thermals," said Sky, watching my carrion birds drift.

Then there was a voice, a curling, spinning voice, a word that was not human. Sky turned to it at once, and reached her hand to me without removing her eyes from the binoculars. She touched my cheek.

She will take her hand away, I thought, when she knows that she has touched you.

But she turned and smiled at me, and before I could smile back or even think, she kissed me, and put her arms around me, her hair closing in around both of us with the wind for a moment, and the scent of her, like cinnamon, quickened me.

The binocular strap tickled the back of my neck. Stay like this, I thought. Forever.

Then she was apart from me, laughing. She handed me the binoculars, and I fumbled with the strap.

The bird sounded its cry again. It did seem amazing to me, as it never really had before, that a hawk could make such a high, science-fiction announcement to all the mice and bugs that it was up there in the sky.

We found a place where we could lie down and gaze upward. The ground was only a little pebbly, and there was grass, and foxtails that were still green. Young eucalyptus trees bent over us, and the shadows of the long, slender leaves spun and danced.

When we stopped waiting for another hawk to skim over us, we held each other, and Sky let me explore her, smiling into me and letting my hand find where it could begin to give her pleasure, although through her clothes, and only for a little while.

I was afraid, really, to do more, or even want more, because even though my body was all over Sky, I was almost disturbed at my good luck, at the way the day had gone, at the way my life had turned and become right.

I was afraid, and yet I wasn't afraid, because I trusted Sky. I knew she would give me what she wanted to give, and what I felt wasn't gratitude and hope so much as ignorance.

She knew everything, and I was just a beginner.

But it was working. I was doing the right things. Tu had told Sky that I was playing baseball again, and I hadn't talked to Jared in what seemed like months.

I actually believed that everything was fine.

And I thought it could last.

———

23

IN MY FATHER'S WORLD there are great spaces that cannot be visited. Sex is one.

He doesn't like to talk about it, and if there is a real sweat-and-grunt scene in a movie you can sense his embarrassment and feel embarrassed yourself. I think, even though it's awkward to consider, that he loved my mother, and that they were happy together in that physical way. But talking about it is to walk off the trail into the woods, and my father will not do that.

He cannot talk about his dead parents, either, although when he does, it is always dignified and beautiful because he talks about them like someone making a speech before serious, quiet people. "My father loved football," he will say. Or "Mom used to love that song," and the statements have a frame around them, a silence that sets them off from conversation.

He cannot talk about many things, and this is strange, because he is easy with words. I have been proud of him when I overhear him on the phone, persuading a tax collector that the factory's tax rates are too high or consoling a man he has had to fire, and doing it so well you know that he has not made an enemy.

I knew there was a conversation coming, a speech he would have to make, and I was embarrassed for him, for both of us, and I did not want to hear it.

I knew what was coming because my mother had taken me to San Francisco, in her new car that smelled of vinyl and adhesive resin, a Japanese sports car she kept stalling on the Bay Bridge.

She had made me wear a tie, and I didn't mind. Feeling uncomfortable suited me that day.

She didn't want to see the wine list, but wanted water, and since there was still officially a drought, a little sign by the ashtray said you had to ask. The water came in very tall glasses like wine glasses, and the ice cubes were flat and small.

She said that we should share a Caesar salad.

"It's fun, coming over here," she said.

It was, although I knew what she was doing—or thought I did. It was a different world, men and women looking like extras in a television show, dressed up and delighted, but quiet, too, knowing not to speak up or spill coffee.

"I don't have to tell you," she said after she had handed our menus to the white-haired waiter. "You know."

My mother has her silences, too. Her silences are tense and dramatic, and make a point.

"You and Dad," I began.

Then her nostrils flared and she had to look away, like

89

someone swallowing a yawn, except it wasn't a yawn.

The tablecloth was coral-pink, and there was a white carnation in the tall, thin vase.

Her voice was steady. "I hope it's okay I brought you over here. I didn't want to talk about it at home."

She had never used exactly that tone of voice with me before—asking if something was okay, one adult to another. "If it makes you feel better," I said, and then I hated myself for sounding so offhand.

She flinched the tiniest bit, and her face was just a little less pretty, the makeup a little too heavy around the eyes. But she recovered very quickly. "You blame me."

I don't know why, but I had to look away and blink back tears. I really couldn't believe what I heard myself saying. "I want everything to be different. I remember when you were happy."

I said this with a twisted voice, with a feeling of sadness so strong it hurt my chest. I stuffed the linen napkin between my teeth, and really hated myself then for losing all control right there in a restaurant, and with zero warning.

I bit the napkin hard.

"Jesus," she said, and leaned on the table with her hands flat.

I imagined what she might be thinking, her silence working on me as it always did.

But she said, "It was unfair to bring you here. I wanted to be in a situation I could control."

I blotted my eyes, wishing I could turn invisible.

"I'm sorry, Stan," she said, and this was new, too, this honest-sounding apology.

I nodded.

WHEN MY FATHER STEPPED HEAVILY up the stairs, I closed my eyes. I knew it all—the long phone call, the long wait before this almost-bedtime visit while he paced downstairs, silently passing from room to room, stalling and facing what was happening at the same time.

I nearly wanted to get out of bed and call down the stairs that he didn't have to talk to me, that he could forget all about it. I knew, I understood, and now I just wanted to pretend it wasn't happening.

But I waited.

When he knocked on the door, and I said, "Come in," I felt that there wasn't enough air. We weren't people, we were cut-outs, cartoons you could pin to a bulletin board.

I saw that my father was dry-eyed. He looked at the room as though deciding it needed to be painted soon.

"She told me she rented an apartment." After I said that, I thought about the words. It sounded simple.

Only when he sat on the bed did he look weary, but weariness was not what I wanted.

He began to say what he had decided to say.

I listened. I saw him being proud, and using his intelligence to reassure me and calm himself, and I felt pity for him.

He loved me, and I felt sorry for him.

24

I COULD SENSE HER in the classroom. I didn't have to turn to look at her. I knew her. I could close my eyes and see.

Mr. Milliken drew a pistol on the board. He took his time scratching in a snub-nosed cap-and-ball. He stood back and nodded once at his work.

"One shot. A lead ball like a nice-sized olive. Right into the back of his head."

Saying such a bad thing made him pause. "It would have made a noise like a balloon popping. A little puff of blue smoke. Just a little puff." Mr. Milliken dusted the chalk from his hands, running his fingers up through the white hair on his arms. "He lived a few hours. But there was no hope. His pillow was soaked with blood."

The bell doesn't sound all at once, simultaneously all over the campus. You hear it down a hall, buzzing in the clock, then trilling outside somewhere.

Sky nudged me on the way by, a swing with her hip that rocked me, and I followed in her wake.

But Mr. Milliken stopped me, a freckled hand closing around my arm. "Are you all right?"

I looked up at his beefy, red face. And for some reason I stayed with him for a moment.

Mr. Milliken hovered, waiting for me to respond.

"Perfect," I said.

"You look old before your time, Stanley. The weight of the world on your shoulders or something." He kept his tone light, so that if I rebuffed him he could act unoffended. "I heard about the baseball team."

I made a little laugh. "That's okay. History," I said, aware just a beat too late that this was not the best word to use.

"I might be able to talk to Mr. O'Brien," said Mr. Milliken. "Put in a good word." His voice went up as he said this, making it sound like a half-question.

I smiled, one corner of my mouth higher than the other: thanks but no thanks. I knew Mr. Milliken was a man who wanted to do good, but I also knew that he lived, basically, in another universe.

"We need to have a nice talk," he said.

"Anytime," I said, in that manner that means "never."

"Before you dig yourself a hole," he said.

TINA RAN OVER A TRASH CAN on Park Boulevard. It was very easy, and looked deliberate.

We drifted, not even going over the speed limit, and then a trash can lid flung itself at the windshield. It bounced away, and then vanished. There was a clattering, a chuffing, a metallic hammering. The car pounded up and down, wrestling, despite its size, with what was trapped beneath it.

Mr. Milliken rose up in his seat, standing on the brake.

When we got out of the car, Tina laughed and leaned against the fender. "I thought I would have a heart attack."

Dung did not laugh. She was chagrined at her friend's driving, and at having to be there on a city street with a squashed trash can.

"I never ran into anything before," said Tina. "My heart is pounding. I thought I was going to die."

Mr. Milliken wrote on his clipboard, and no one came forth to claim the trash can, which was not on the sidewalk anymore, but out in the street.

"We can sue them, right?" said Tina. "We can sue them for leaving their trash can all over the place."

Mr. Milliken finished writing and stuck a Post-it on the can.

Then, looking completely satisfied with life, he said, "Let's go run over something else."

JARED SAW ME at my locker. He didn't say anything. He just looked at me and made his silent laugh.

I dropped my eyes, and felt myself blush, and it wasn't until then that I knew how much I had wanted to avoid him.

"I'll call you tonight," I shouted through the metallic din.

His eyes brightened, and he turned away.

Jared likes me, I told myself. He likes me and he needs me.

I had let him down, and he had been waiting for me. I reflected on what I had just called to him. Those were not the words I wanted to say, but the words had uttered themselves.

The air conditioning broke down just after school. The

94

halls were hot and stuffy. An air-quality study had reported the school to have the lowest possible quality of breathable air, and that was when everything was humming. Now, with the air stagnant, we began to drag ourselves through the thickening atmosphere. There had been a fight during sixth period, but I had not heard the complete story. There was a handful of hair across from Mr. Milliken's door, torn out of someone's head, even though you couldn't see any blood.

I knocked. There was no answer. I tried the door, but the knob would not turn. He might be in there, I reasoned, correcting papers, ignoring the din from the hall, or even unable to hear.

The teachers all locked their doors, even during class, ever since the year before, when a French teacher had been attacked by someone with a knife. Her throat had been cut, but not very badly. You couldn't even see a scar.

I knocked again, but by then it was too hot.

I STOPPED BY SKY'S HOUSE, and as always she was not home. Tu had jacked the big white car up onto four wooden blocks. The car had no tires, and only ugly black steel stumps where the wheels should be. He was under the car, looking up into it.

"All kinds of trouble," he said cheerfully.

———

25

I DIDN'T CALL JARED that night. It wasn't because I forgot—
I deliberately did not.

I made my father and myself microwave-toastable fish and
chips—Iceland cod. My mother called, and she sounded
cautious and rested, a combination that left me guessing how
she really felt about my father and myself. She had a view
of the Golden Gate Bridge, and a little patio. There were
tennis courts. She was going to buy a geranium.

"And you come over and visit," she said, and I was wondering if she meant: and start moving in, and get away from
your father.

Because despite what she had said, I knew she felt I belonged with her. Even though she would be gone most of
the time. Even though she would wait for me to ask her how
was Honolulu or how was Tahoe all the time.

It was another one of those things you could see without
talking about it. This was going to change. My father knew,
and I knew.

He overheard the conversation. When it was over, he
looked up from the manual to the new computer he had just
bought and said, "She's okay?"

I said she was, but it was like two people talking about bad
weather. It was terrible, but beyond us, out of our power.

And then we looked at each other, and he smiled. It was almost a joke. His silence glowed in him, making him sweat and reflect the light from the television. It was terrible, and we couldn't really say anything about it.

So I didn't call Jared, on purpose, every moment that passed a moment in which Jared was waiting, a moment in which he would know I wanted out of the game and that I was leaving whether he wanted me to or not.

I WOKE DURING THE NIGHT after very broken sleep. I heard that whisper in the air I associate with falling rain. I sat holding my breath.

Wrong. There is something wrong.

Almost like one of those times I must have heard my parents making love and woke up, almost crying out. Maybe I had cried out in the middle of it, I thought. Maybe my little baby self had bawled and interrupted them.

My father used to pretend to be a bear. He used to make her happy. I crippled their marriage.

When I slipped from the bed and looked out the window, there was nothing.

I called his name in a low voice, the two syllables not like a name at all, but a magical incantation, a word intended to break a spell.

Jared was here, somewhere. Somewhere in the house, and that whisper, that fine, high noise, had been his step.

He needs you, said the fanged voice in me. He needs you, and he won't let you go.

97

26

Jared was sitting up very high, at the last level of the nearly empty football stands. And he was talking to Sky.

It was morning, the stands blistered with dew. I was warm inside, almost happy, to see the two of them together, and bounded up the flat, flaking seats of the stands, but as I leaped upward I felt the tiniest hook inside me, in my chest.

I didn't like it. I didn't like the way he was turned to look at her, and the way she was studying his face, calm and entirely focused on him.

I made myself spring upward all the faster, my shoes squeaking on the wet yellow planks. I called to Jared, and he turned to look down with a smile.

When I joined them, I was winded for a moment and could not speak.

"I was just talking to Sky," said Jared.

I looked from one to the other, breathing hard, with what I knew must be the wrong sort of smile.

"I was telling her," Jared continued, in the tone he would use to tell a wonderful piece of news, "about our game."

As I fought my way into being able to speak, Sky cut me off with her look.

Jared laughed that wonderful quiet laugh. "She doesn't believe me. I bare my soul and she turns the channel."

"Stanley," she said, slowly, carefully. "I know the kind of person you are."

"Go ahead," said Jared. "Believe whatever you want."

I put my hands on my hips. Why shouldn't I, I told myself. Why not? I had always believed in the truth.

But I knew the next words would be important, and could change everything about the way Sky felt about me. Say the right thing, I told myself. Lie. You have nothing to hide, of course, not really.

Tell a lie. Deny it.

I could lie to anyone. My dad. My mom. I could tell a dressed-up version of the truth to Jared. He would see through it, of course, but the attempt was possible. But to Sky I could tell only the truth.

I took a deep breath. "We play a game," I said.

"A game." Her voice was low and serious, and her eyes were steady.

"I told her the plain truth," said Jared, because he knew: I was hoping, for an instant, that he had told her an exaggeration that I could at least partly deny. "Just the truth."

She stood. She put her hand on my arm as she stepped down, and I touched the place on my shirt where her hand had rested. I sensed her steps all the way down, communicated through the struts and timbers of the stands.

Jared narrowed his eyes and gave me a half-smile.

I sat slowly, the wet soaking into my seat.

"This is not your type of woman," said Jared.

I was not looking at Jared. I was gazing down at the figures crossing the football field. One of them was Sky. My eyes followed her all the way to the building. "I like her a lot," my numb voice said.

"She is beautiful," he said, and I turned, ready to be offended even at Jared if he said anything obscene or crude about Sky. But Jared was sensitive, serious. He nodded reassurance. "She is. Big, slow, and serene."

Maybe he liked her. Maybe he wanted her. The thoughts pricked me.

"Not my type," he said, almost dreamily.

For a long moment, I could not ask the next question.

"Were you in my house last night, Jared?"

Jared made one of his gestures, both "I might have been" and "what difference does it make?" His cigarette made a wreath of smoke, and I could not bear to look at Jared anymore.

"You don't have any business going into my father's house."

I was surprised at these words, but glad I had said them.

"Poor Stan. You're upset," Jared said after a long while, and I could tell that he had been waiting for me to speak, and did not like having to make the first move. "I've been very generous with you, Stanley."

I must have shaken my head, or hunched away from him. Somehow my body said no.

"I let you share my secret. I openly shared it with you. You were like a brother."

Don't say anything, I told myself. Don't let him draw you into any sort of argument. He's smart—much smarter than you are.

100

His voice sounded gentle. "I don't really mind that you ran away and left me in the house. But you mind. You can't stand it."

I must have shaken my head once again and looked away, because Jared's next words were the ugliest-sounding words I had ever heard him use. "I'm never going to let you forget how cowardly you were. I thought it was funny. But you didn't."

He stubbed his cigarette out on one of the boltheads, and stood.

The bell rang, yet no one moved from the field below, preferring to talk to each other, laugh, thump a soccer ball back and forth.

"It's all right," he said. "I'm sorry."

This was new. I glanced up at him. He was being clever, pretending to apologize.

He read my suspicion. He made a little smile. "Go on and be dead, Stanley. It doesn't matter to me."

And he left me. Just like that, striding down the bleachers in no special hurry.

I was rounded up in a hall sweep. Mr. Hawking, a strong former convict who ran our security, laughed when he saw me. It was not a mean laugh. He was a handsome black man, and liked the way I used to play baseball, and had always kidded me about throwing my face into the ball.

Now he just said, "Got to be quicker than this, Stanley," and herded me along with a group of other students into the dean's office, where we all sat until the dean called in to say that his car battery had been stolen and he wouldn't be coming in.

We all got passes, and I cruised into French in time to take a test, one of those stretches of the French language in which you say things about the valise of Madame Duboise and the letter that was on the table having been removed by the young girl. I wondered who were these French people with their travel plans and their homes full of messages and servants.

Sky finished the test first. I could hear her cap her pen.

The test had pictures. I was supposed to write a commentary on the pictures in French. I leaned forward and did the best I could, but it was hard to concentrate.

I had a plan—a way out. It would silence Jared, and it would finish the game.

27

I WATCHED THE HOUSE with green shutters and three chimneys carefully.

I watched it in the early morning, taking a detour on the way to school. I watched it from the alley in the evening. I knew who lived there without knowing anything, just as I knew the characters in the French book, or the man whose leg was sheared off by a crocodile. I knew nothing. I knew enough.

The owner was a man, slightly out of shape, and his younger wife. Or at least, she was pretty and the man was not all that handsome. He waddled a little bit when he came down the walkway to pluck the newspaper off the lawn, but he often seemed to be whistling through his lower teeth, the sort of whistling I think means contentment. He was even a little smug. His life was complete.

She flounced as she walked. He drove an Audi, and she drove a Fiat, and there was a little girl who visited sometimes, a daughter, I decided, from an earlier marriage.

They probably saw intruders as a compliment: someone thinks we're rich enough to rob.

It took a week. Not more. I knew enough about them to write a research paper. They got a lot of bills, the kind with window envelopes that are green or sand-yellow so you have to give them a second look. They took the *Examiner* and the *Tribune*.

Once he saw me, looked right at me, as I wandered by across the street. His eyes caught mine. They were easy on me, dismissing me. He was probably the kind of man who would be reassured that I was a white kid, and harmless-looking. But then he looked at me just a beat too long, and my spine went cold.

I smiled. Just a little smile, a crinkling of the eyes, a casual I'm-on-my-way attitude.

After another beat, he smiled back.

They had a lot of friends. Tanned, square-jawed men dropped him off after tennis, and I wondered if he might be more fit than he looked, or perhaps very likeable. She jogged with friends, wearing a white terry-cloth visor, a visor so white I knew that she must replace it every week or two.

I had a plan, but I didn't know when the plan would begin to establish itself. I was an explorer not sure on what island he would build his fort. I felt uncertain but fresh, eager. I could not be sure of anything, and that made me begin to feel alive.

Sky saw me in class, but her smile was sad, and when I tried to speak to her, she only tilted her head, smiling but looking away.

I passed Jared in the hall, and he gazed through me. He looked pale and gaunt, and missed more school, showing up late to classes, looking both bored and triumphant. I knew that he was, in a way, pleased that I had quit.

He had won a contest I had not been aware we were playing. I had thought we were partners. But Jared had always been out to prove that I was inferior. The game had been called, in Jared's mind, Stanley the Loser. I had lived up to his expectations.

Now I had a surprise.

———

28

I DIDN'T KNOW WHICH NIGHT it would be, but I knew that the night would come. I was more and more certain every time I hurried through the dark, and felt myself becoming more and more invisible, fading, growing transparent.

I was free of the world of clocks and history tests. But I intended no harm. I did not want to take anything of value. I only wanted to achieve that single, perfect moment of life, and then I could stop. Jared thought he had taught me all of this. Of course, in a way, he had. But I could master an aspect of the game he would never achieve.

IT WAS JUST ANOTHER EVENING. There was nothing to tell me that this was the night. I escaped out my bedroom window with the ease of someone going to work or school. I felt like one of those race car drivers who never open the car door, but always swing out the window.

My father was no threat. It was entirely safe. We lived like two men who liked each other but did not quite share the same language. The pidgin silence my father had always used had broken down into plain quiet. My father would never check on me.

I scrambled down the roof slope, and leaped to the damp lawn.

I didn't go directly to the house with green shutters. I went by the school, and saw the new buildings all lit up for the maintenance crews and the security, and I stayed wide of all the lights because of the school police car that was backed up to the cafeteria loading bay.

Computers were always getting stolen, and the cops were supposed to be cracking down, but everybody said that it was people on the inside, custodial or maintenance or cops, and that nobody could stop what was happening.

I remembered the night the school blew up. It had been a gas leak. An old main had fractured spontaneously, the result of minor earthquakes, and not so minor ones, over eighty or ninety years, and the result of something else, too, gravity and time—the way things are.

People still talked about it. The school blew up so badly the news was sure it was a bomb, and the cops had dropped by and were very polite to my father and went away almost at once when he called the company lawyer. But they had questioned everybody, and people from the federal government did, too, Tobacco and Firearm men measuring how far a doorknob had blown across MacArthur Boulevard.

The gas had trickled out into the corridors past the showers, and into the dance studio, all the old closets and storage rooms. It had been a school of spires and towers. No one had ever really looked at it. It was the kind of building you remembered more than saw even when it was there.

It had turned inside out.

We had all gone to see it, towel racks and clock faces and all the amazing debris blown all the way across the drug corner. Yellow police tape had trembled in the sunlight, but it couldn't protect the junk from being pawed through.

I jogged away from the glow of the school lights, and zigzagged across the street to avoid streetlights. I knew how to do it, that slow sprint, an easy lope, a way of hurrying without seeming to be traveling fast, a way of remaining secret without hiding.

I hurried along the sidewalk, over the tree roots twisted in the squares of concrete. I was just dancing over such a root when I saw. And stood still.

There was an extra car in the driveway. I nearly fell to the ground right then. This was the night. This was the very night I had been planning for.

And I was almost too late.

The guests were already in the driveway, that after-dinner good-bye ceremony that can take so long, people promising to see each other some other time. *Keep talking*, I whispered. *Gossip all you want.*

I turned and tried not to run, and tried to still my heart. It's all right, I told myself. Don't panic. This is exactly what you knew would happen.

I'm brilliant, I told myself.

The alley was so familiar that the sound of my steps in the fine gravel was almost pleasant.

The dog Jared had soothed that night rarely barked, but

tonight he decided to use his voice. It was not a bark—more of a throat clearing. I hushed him, and my stage whisper broke another bark from him, but it was half-hearted. He remembered.

The splintered top of the fence rasped under my palms. I was over the fence and into the backyard easily.

A car door clunked. An engine chattered and caught. I was running out of time.

The back door was chained. The kitchen windows each lifted a finger width and jammed. *You have no time—hurry. You have plenty of time—don't blunder.*

The laundry window jammed.

I forced my shoulder against it, and it shuddered upward another creak or two, but jammed again.

The distant front door shut. The subtle shift and rustle of an occupied house was at my ear. The man spoke. The woman answered. Then she answered too close, from the kitchen, perhaps, or even just inside the laundry room.

I told myself not to duck my head or make any quick movement. Easy and smooth, I told myself.

When the back door opened, I dropped to the grass.

———

29

I CROUCHED, breathing so hard it hurt.

My eyes picked up the woman, fading at the edge of the back porch light. Her steps were in the grass. Her figure was bent slightly to one side, and I caught the plastic rustle of a garbage sack.

I slipped through the back door.

Inside, the air was warm, a mass of cooking odors. The kitchen was a mess of dirty dishes, casserole dishes of meatballs and steamers of broccoli. On a butcher table stood several bottles of liquor.

I could not move my feet. I was standing there gawking at someone's kitchen while a step was in the hall, the step of the man, slow and weighty, and the intake of breath as the owner of the house was about to speak.

Get small, I told myself. Get invisible.

The purr of the water heater was a welcome sound. The scent of detergent and the barely discernable waft of bleach were my refuge. I slid to a crouch behind the water heater, and took long breaths to still myself.

Water surged in the sink, and there was the friendly clunk of dishes in water. They weren't talking to each other, tired, comfortable. The garbage disposal grumbled and water splashed. The disposal worked a long time.

When it was silent, the man splashed more water and shifted his weight, and the dishes clattered one by one into the rack. Once the heater at my ear thundered, and the laundry room floor was blue from the gas fire under the heater.

If they don't see you, you aren't there, and they won't see you if you are perfectly still.

It was a shock when the kitchen light went out. I cautioned myself, actually moving my lips: don't move.

The longer I stayed motionless, the easier it became. The tank of water gave warmth, and I belonged right where I was. I had a giddy feeling of security. Everything was fine. They were upstairs, and I was here.

But it couldn't last.

I knew that before he went to bed the man, who was wary enough to have a gun beside his bed, would be cautious enough to turn on the silent alarm. As soon as I began to move, the space sensor would see me, and I would not be invisible anymore.

I began to stand up. Very slowly, my knee joint popping.

I was up, and now the device in the hall would begin to register my movement.

The floor made too much noise. It had been waxed again, and my running shoes squeaked on the surface. I crouched at the entrance to the hallway, and the red light was on.

There was no time.

It was already too late.

And I had convinced myself how brilliant I was.

The alarm in the hall made the tiniest tick, hardly a sound at all. And I knew that it would happen all over again.

Only this time it would be worse.

30

DEAD MEAT, said the old, mean voice in me.

You.

You don't have a chance.

My foot slipped with another squeal, and then the carpet muffled my steps, and even though I willed myself quiet, the carpet clung to me, each step a heavy clump.

The plumbing in the walls, in the ceiling, thrummed, or perhaps that steady, distant rushing sound was the blood in my arteries.

There was a very heavy weight inside me, in my belly. I had to pee.

I wasn't sneaking across the floor, I was wading, and my guts were growling. All this noise made it impossible to pretend, and by the time I was on the stairs I did not bother to be light-footed. It didn't matter. They must have heard me by now. The only thing that mattered now was speed.

Each step was loose, a wagging, warped board. Each nail

in the stairway made a little shriek. I gave up all attempt at quiet, stormed up the remaining steps, and dived toward the doorway to the bedroom.

I had the exact picture, just then, of where they were. Under the bathroom door down the hall was a sliver of light, and that rushing sound was bath water. And there was only one of them in the bedroom, only one, and it was the woman.

I saw all this, the walls transparent to me. And then I was in the bedroom, in the bright light, every lamp in the room lit, and the woman's eyes went wide, and her breath caught.

She screamed.

It was her scream that stunned me. I went dumb. I couldn't think. My hand seized the first thing within reach, acting on its own, both dumb and quick, and her screams pulsed through me.

I was slowing down, wading through the room. My bones would not lift. My feet dragged. I would never make it back to the doorway again.

We stayed like that forever. The woman, one small breast just exposed, a tangle of clothing held up as a shield, did not look human. Her face was too afraid, her lipstick too dark, way too dark, nearly black against the pallor of her skin.

"It's all right," I nearly said. I moved my lips. I all but uttered the words. "It's all right. I won't hurt you."

But I did not speak. I had no voice. I had my prize, a lump of some sort in my fist, and I reached the doorway and the stairwell just as the man swung naked and wet, a great hairless dripping bear, out of the bathroom.

He didn't say a word, or make a sound, and that's what made it worse. His wet feet slapped the floor, slapped a stair, his genitals hidden in a wet mass of black hair, the coursing hair down his belly skimming the big dome of his fat.

I had the sense, as a little boy would, that this large male animal was powerful and ugly but also somehow right. I felt myself slowing down, taking a step a little too slowly, so he could catch me. I wanted him to catch me. I wanted his hand on my neck, because he was right. I was his if he wanted me.

His wet, hairy hands slipped around either side of my face from behind, and the weight of him, the dripping bulk, fell down and over me, a wave of human meat.

I closed my eyes and went down, rolling from step to step, shoulder, hip, ribs shaken with each bounce.

But I was rolling lightly, my body knowing what to do, and he crashed. The struts of the banister broke, and the banister itself reared up in the dim light. One of the man's joints, a shoulder or a knee, snapped.

He said something I didn't understand, a word in a foreign language, sliding farther down the stairs as I turned, running now, escaping across the living room.

I was turning back, unable to control my body.

Stay here, my body said. He's hurt. You can't run away.

A whipcrack deafened me. My hearing was gone. The sound of my breath, my heartbeat, the thud of my feet—it was all gone. There was nothing.

There was the sight of the woman on the stairs as I turned back. She crouched at the top of the stairs, both hands together. She was taking aim again, and she knew exactly what to do, her feet speared, her hands bringing up the weapon as I turned away, tingling within, my lungs burning, my flesh alive in the places that would soon explode.

I dived through the curtain, through the glass, into the world.

31

RUNNING, LUNGS EMPTY OF AIR, I knew I was dead. I even wanted it—an end to it all.

The thing I carried was fat and heavy. I would not look at it, or let myself really see what it was I had stolen.

They'll catch me and it will all be over.

But I reached my own backyard, and climbed upward into my own house.

"Stanley."

A single word. I couldn't breathe.

My father was sitting on my bed when I crawled up the slope of the roof, through the window, and spilled onto the floor. The light was not on, and he must have been sitting in the dark for a long time, because when he said my name it came out hoarse, like a voice that has been tense and silent for a long time.

Then, his voice clear and strong, "Where have you been?"

My lips couldn't form a single word. I tried. I wanted to lie. I even wanted to tell the truth.

He grabbed me, pulled me to my feet, and shook me. He shook me hard, and it hurt. "Where have you been, Stanley?" he yelled.

He flung me away, and I stumbled into my chair, which rocked and nearly went over.

He put his hands to his face, and bent over. I wanted to tell him it was all right. I wanted to tell him everything was perfectly fine.

"You're doing something wrong." He was panting heavily, as though he had been running through the darkness.

Tell him something, my inner voice said. Don't just sit there.

I huddled in the chair. My feelings made me a cripple. And besides, I had something to hide now, something in the pocket of my pants. It was something that had to be a secret, always.

"Stanley." He said the name again, and while I knew that the name was mine, it sounded spooky, a word with a nasty rasp to it.

My father doesn't like to show anger. He knows that sometimes the words plunge out when you are mad and you can't stop them. He resented me for making him angry, as well as for making him worry. I tried to formulate an apology, an explanation.

"You're doing something," he whispered. "I don't know what it is."

115

But some of his force was gone now. He had begun to think, consider, reflect.

I was shivering.

He turned, moving woodenly. He found the lamp and fumbled with it. The button clicked but the light wouldn't come on. When it did at last, it was too bright, and we both looked away, blinking.

The effort to adjust to the light calmed him a little bit more. "I thought," he said, measuring his words, "you went off somewhere with your mother." He made a bitter little whisper-laugh through his teeth. "I tried calling her."

But she's not home, I thought, filling in the silence with the words I knew he wanted to speak: she's gone, and I had to sit here waiting.

He said, "Is that what you want?"

I had my arms folded, my face turned away, one shoulder up. His question didn't make any sense for a moment.

"Would you be happier with her?"

I had to piece the meaning together, like translating French. No, I thought. The thought shivered me. Not that I would be unhappy living with my mother. It shook me that he knew so little about me.

"You're hurt."

I stirred, as though waking. No, I thought, not hurt. I'm fine.

"Jesus, Stan. What have you been doing?"

It wasn't anger anymore. It was something else. Curiosity, worry, pain at the sight of my pain.

32

IT WAS EARLY.

I had fallen into a gray, awkward sleep, and when I woke, I sensed my father's wakefulness far away. Even that next morning, in the gray light, I thought that I could tell my father. There was still time. I could tell him what I had done.

But I listened to the sounds of my father getting up and I knew I couldn't tell him about breaking the glass, me cascading with the window to the ground, and rolling, stunned and yet still moving.

I couldn't tell him about running, snot and blood streaming from my nose, running until the stitch in my side bent me double. And how I had run even then, running blinking back tears, half hoping sleepers would wake at the sound of me and call the police so it could all be over.

But it wasn't over. It was only beginning.

I wasn't hurt, not really. There was blood in my nostrils, a sort of red grit, and a cut on my neck that looked like a cat scratch, or a love bite. My muscles ached, and there was a soreness inside my belly, which I knew would never accept food again, not after last night's nausea.

I had slept on the lump, keeping it under my pillow. I wouldn't even let myself look at it, the stolen trophy, the thing my hand had fallen on while the woman's eyes opened so wide and she began to scream. If only she had been quiet.

But it was my own bad luck, my own impetuous dumbness, that had accomplished this.

I was a thief.

Maybe I didn't really have it. Maybe I hadn't taken it.

I lifted the bunched pillow, and an object was there, a secret wrapped in an undershirt. I picked up the loose bundle, and weighed it in my hands. Surely it's not what I think it is. I'll look and it will be entirely different.

I let the cotton cloth fall away.

It was true.

I had really done it.

It was a woman's wallet, and in that glossy leather with the half-worn embossed gold stars, I had taken some hope. A man's wallet would have been unmistakable, but I had tried to convince myself during the night that this item was a diary or a makeup kit, some booklet or clutch that snapped shut with a strap but wasn't full of money and credit cards.

It fell open as I unsnapped it, because it was so full and had been used so many times that it was easy for it to yield and open up, crammed with currency and smiling pictures of older relatives and an elementary-school picture of a little girl with a retainer on her teeth.

I had stolen her wallet.

I wanted to cough a dry-mouthed laugh. Hey, wait a minute. This was a mistake. I didn't really steal this. My hand did.

But it's done, I told myself. It's done. And I had a new

plan, a very good one, one that made sense and would settle everything completely.

There was a bang downstairs. I froze.

Only a lid off a pot, I told myself. But that reminded me of my father. Any moment he could come up the stairs.

I hid the wallet in the only place I could be sure of, the only place I could sense every moment: the front pocket of my pants. They were baggy, drab brown pants, with deep pockets. The wallet dropped all the way in, and stayed there.

Any second my father could be at the bedroom door, knocking, peering in, wanting to continue that talk I knew he had broken off because he needed time to think of the right words.

He had taken the time. He would have his little speech ready.

I was trembling, and my breath made a grunt when it came out of me, but I was capable. I could handle this situation. I don't panic. When my ligament had torn and I lay there on the infield, looking up at the sky, I had even tried to make a joke. I hadn't been able to think of one, it's true, but I had been working on it. I could fix things, even now.

I would give this to Jared.

I would say that this was proof that I wasn't afraid. This was the trophy from the last time I played the game. I had improved the game, I would say. I had stretched it from stealing socks and cigarette lighters to something really big.

I closed my eyes and I felt like I was falling.

33

BUT THE WALLET STAYED WITH ME all day, and I never saw Jared. I would see a figure slip around a corner and I would call out and it would turn out to be someone else entirely.

Jared was not there, and the wallet was still mine.

The results of the French test were a disaster. I had done especially poorly on the back page, where there was a mimeographed drawing of a woman arranging flowers on a table, a valise in the background.

"Iron spikes driven by sheer muscle power," said Mr. Milliken. "An entire railroad laid by human might." He paused beside my desk, and smiled, in a sad way I think I could understand.

"People died," he announced, as though suddenly remembering it all. "Plunged into gorges. Crushed in avalanches. Chinese people!" he exclaimed.

We wrote and doodled and the headlines continued, the revolver perfected, the cattle driven, barbed wire contrived, the nineteenth century being hurried, swept along under the headings CUSTER BUTCHERED and INDIANS FREEZE TO DEATH.

And all I wanted in the world was to slip the wallet into Jared's hands and say, "Here it is. I took it. You take it back."

All I wanted was to have a life again.

34

Tu LAUGHED WHEN HE SAW ME, but it was an open, easy greeting. He scooted out just a bit from under the big white Chevy, which was still on blocks and did not seem likely to go anywhere on this afternoon. "Not here," he said. "Volleyball."

"That's all right," I said, trying not to sound disappointed.

"She's coming home soon. I want to surprise her. I'm going to have this car ready."

"It doesn't look all that ready, Tu." It still didn't even have wheels.

"You can help," he said.

"I doubt it."

"You have good hands, Stanley. Just the right touch. This is too much, you know. Too much for one person to do."

"I don't think you need my help," I said, and I was already starting to fade away a bit, out toward the sidewalk. Tu was busy, and Sky was gone, and the wallet weighed in my pocket, warm and fat.

"You think I can do everything all by myself," said Tu cheerfully from under the car.

"Just about."

I stayed where I was, kept by the possibility that I could, indeed, help Tu.

121

"I need the wrench from inside the car," he said, his voice muffled by the car, rising up from under it and within it, taking on a far-off metallic timbre.

I opened the car door. His request was complicated. There was the familiar ratchet wrench, glittering on the worn-out floor mat. There was a tool chest, an open box with a wooden handle. There was a grimy wrench, gigantic, with a red handle. I gathered all the tools, clambering into the car. There were even crescent wrenches in the toolbox, I saw, slender and looking too small to be useful here.

I swung the car door shut and crouched beside the car. "Which one?" I asked, feeling ignorant, but satisfied that I had every wrench possible.

We both sensed it. There was no sound at all, except for the slightest chuckling noise, and the slightest sensation in my vision that maybe I was just a little dizzy because the world wasn't steady.

Tu scrambled out from under the big car and we both gazed at the car, waiting. It inched forward on its blocks, and it was about to fall.

I didn't want to move, or make a sound that might cause the car to shift forward, and bring it down on the driveway.

From somewhere within the car, there was the tiniest creak, a spring settling, or a hinge deciding to stay where it was.

Tu smiled. "It's not safe!" he said. "It could fall at any moment, Stanley." He said this cheerfully. "But I'll fix it."

Tu strode into the depths of the garage to drag forth a jack, a large black contraption on wheels.

He laughed at the expression on my face. "Don't worry, Stanley."

When I knew that the car was safe, I left Tu, hurrying, feeling that every moment I did not see Jared, the wallet was growing heavier.

35

No one answered the door at Jared's house. I listened hard, and rang the bell again, but the house was empty.

When I reached my own house, I called Jared's number, but there was no answer.

The wallet slipped from my fingers as I tugged open my dresser. A gold-colored Capwell's card slipped out of the wallet, and I pushed the card back where it belonged, and found a place for the wallet among my socks.

All evening I tried to call Jared.

There was never an answer, and I wasn't hungry, and I didn't want to do anything but hear Jared's voice.

I couldn't eat. I unwrapped a candy bar and left it untouched.

I was wide awake when my father came home late. I heard his car, and the distant rasp of his door key. I hurried downstairs to see him opening a carton of orange juice.

He did not speak to me for a moment, letting silence settle around us. But his eyes were aware, watching, knowing. "What's wrong?" he said.

The words were hard to say. "I wanted to make sure you were all right."

My father opened the refrigerator, and turned to look at me, and I could see that he took my remark seriously, and did not want to turn it aside with a casual remark of his own. "Just the usual sort of day," he said, but he did not mean this lightly. "No accidents."

"You were so late," I said.

He shut the refrigerator. "No later than usual," he said. He made a little movement of his head, as though consulting a clock in his mind. "Well, maybe a little."

He seemed touched that I had worried about him, but puzzled, too. "Are you afraid of something, Stanley?"

"No," I said. "I'm not afraid." That's the kind of statement I would usually make with a laugh, or some sort of reassuring expression. But I said it with a dry, tight voice.

"I think I'll open a can of chili," he said, opening the cupboard, and turning back to me.

I could tell that he wanted me to sit down and eat with him. But I said that I wasn't hungry, and went upstairs in the dark to lie down.

Knowing there was something wrong.

————

36

JARED CAME TO SEE ME in the middle of a desert of silence.

I sat up, surprised that I had fallen asleep.

There was something wrong. He looked taller than I had remembered him, and he moved quickly, pulling my desk chair out just a little so he could sit.

He was sitting so that he was a silhouette, a figure of blank black against the gray light from the window. He was plainly waiting for me to speak.

"I was worried," I said.

"Why?" he said, with some amusement.

When I didn't answer, he said, "What did you steal?"

I met his eyes. "I wanted to impress you."

"I don't think you really understood the game, Stanley."

I was angry then. I understood enough. I tried to get out of bed, but Jared was on his feet. He touched me very gently on my shoulder. It was one of those gestures that he had mastered, one that said so many things at once. Be calm, it said. Everything is all right. It also said that something was over. Something was finished.

"They drink, did you know that?" he said.

I didn't answer.

"The people with the green shutters are lushes." He laughed soundlessly. "We thought we were so smooth."

Then his manner changed. He watched me for a while as though to judge me, or remember my face for a long time afterward.

"You never wear the socks, do you?"

I blinked a question.

"The socks I stole. You should wear them. For good luck."

I WOKE.

There was too much sun. I would be late for first period. And yet, as I climbed out of bed, I was aware of a sound I had been hearing in my sleep. It was trilling again, and he was answering it.

I sensed my father's step in the house, sensed his voice, all but inaudible through the walls, through the floor as he answered the phone.

Why hasn't he gone to work? I thought. He'll be late, too.

I pulled on an undershirt and stumbled to the open window. Jared, I thought, as though my thoughts could communicate themselves to him. Jared, you shouldn't sneak into my father's house.

But I didn't mean it, really—not this time.

I had been worried over nothing.

I dressed with more care than usual, putting on a shirt I almost never wear, a green one with long sleeves. And I tied my shoelaces before going downstairs, something I don't often do.

The wallet, I thought. Why didn't I give him the wallet?

I came down the stairs, and entered the kitchen, and when

I saw my father's eyes, I knew that something terrible had happened.

37

MY FATHER MOVED A SPOON from one place to another on the counter, and did not want to say anything for a moment.

He gave a small cough. "I have some bad news about Jared," he said.

The kitchen seemed big, as big as a place that was expanding, walls moving outward, the toaster and the metal frame of the microwave bright and clear.

My father was waiting, as though I had to give him permission to say anything more.

If I never make a sound, and never move again, I told myself, everything will be all right. But I asked, in a voice like a whisper, "What happened?"

"He fell onto the freeway."

The words made no sense, as though the sounds fell apart and became nonsense as soon as my father said them. Surely that's not what my father really said, I thought. Surely my ears made a mistake.

But my voice, alive on its own, was making a sound. "He fell?" I heard it ask.

My father came over to me and put his arms around me, and his own voice was tight with feeling when he said, "Jared's dead."

So this is what I do, I thought, when I don't know what to think or feel. I stand here, looking around at the place where I live, in the morning sunlight, seeing and feeling nothing at all. Nothing at all, except confusion. Very great confusion.

I wanted to be far away. I wanted today to be a day years ago, far off from what was happening.

Then I felt myself moving, stepping toward the stairs. My hand slid along the banister. Each step was heavy, and I was not certain I would ever be able to reach the top, and step into my bedroom.

But when I was there, I pulled open the dresser drawer.

It was still there.

On a morning like this, I was no longer certain what would continue to exist, and what would not. But the wallet was still there, a weight in my hand.

My body knew what to do. It stepped down the stairs, cradling the wallet in one hand. I carried it like a thing that could break easily, at a rough movement, or even a harsh sound.

I carried it into the kitchen. It looked worn in the morning light, a woman's wallet that was far from new, smooth and frayed at one corner.

I put the wallet on the counter and my father looked at it, and then raised his eyes and looked at me.

Waiting for me to speak.

38

SOMETIMES THE SUN IS IN YOUR EYES and you can't see. You just have to know.

At the last instant the ball is there, the stitches dark red against the scuff, the leather marred and stained, and the bat knows what to do, and the body.

I swung, all the way around, and I could feel the sour note all the way up the bat, into my arms. The ball bounced twice and Tu caught it in his hand, the one without the glove.

"Hit it harder, Stanley," he said.

The next pitch was high, and floated in on me, and I fell out of the way.

I got up and didn't bother brushing myself off. With Tu pitching, I had to get out of the way a lot. I gave him a look that said: throw it straight.

"It's not so easy," he said.

"You're going great," I called, to encourage him.

The field was empty except for the two of us, baseball season over, summer vacation already begun. I was careful not to look out across center field, across the faded stripes of the football games, into the empty stands.

Tu threw the ball at my feet, the yellow streak bounding, the backstop taking the ball and stirring all along its frame.

Tu stooped and chose another ball from the green garbage bag of them at his feet. It was a deal: I would help him learn how to pitch, and he would give me the chance to work on my swing. We worked alone in the field, and when the garbage bag was empty, we both went out to collect the balls and started all over again.

Tu kneaded the ball, something he must have learned from watching television, and I waited.

My father had visited the house with the green shutters, and had left the wallet with the man and the woman who lived there.

"I talked to them," was all he would say about it.

When I had asked him what he had said, and why they wouldn't talk to the police, he looked at me, into my eyes, and said, "It's over."

But it wasn't over. The game was over, and Jared was gone, but there was nothing left to take the place of the way I had felt.

I had felt alive because of Jared.

I hit it hard, and the ball made a sound that was high and sweet off the bat. I leaned forward, holding my breath. It didn't touch the grass until it reached the dried-up places in the field, and then it bounced, up into the stands.

I didn't look away in time. The ball bounded on the hard, flat seats of the bleachers. It took an especially high bounce off one of the boltheads, and it stopped near where Jared had always sat, watching me, mocking me at a distance, guiding me back to him.

"It's a home run, Stanley," said Tu, clapping, a one-man crowd. "Run the bases, Stanley, don't just stand there."

I shook my head. The empty stands were a presence, a thing that knew me.

Tu was calling, but I didn't move. It was silly to run the bases there in the open field, no one watching, nothing but two people practicing.

"Run the bases, Stanley. You hit the ball, you run!"

I shook my head again, and then I dropped the bat.

Something about Tu, and his smile, and the way the bat rolled away made me start to skip down the first-base path.

"A home run for Stanley!" called Tu, like an announcer or a coach, waving me around the bases like a trainer celebrating in the midst of a crowd.

I began to trot, beyond first base, toward second, the flattened canvas bag we were using as second base slipping slightly under my foot as I ran, taking my time, making the moment last, the silence watching me, the emptiness looking on as I stepped home.